PUSH!

Close Encounters of The Midwife Kind

By

Sylvia Baddeley

Very best Regards,

Sylvia.

For Pat, Gwyneth, Helen, Marian, Yvonne, Penny, and Lesley; the Nineteen Seventy-Two Set.

ACKNOWLEDGEMENTS

My thanks to William Cooke for his support and continuing encouragement and to Saffron, my lovely next door neighbour, one of whose babies was my last delivery. Watching both of your daughters grow up and reminiscing with you is a continual reminder of how lucky I was to work in a profession that fulfilled me completely. And many thanks to Pat and Melvyn Williams whose enthusiasm sustained me throughout.

CONTENTS

Prelude

Filled with apprehension on her first day of training at the local maternity hospital, student midwife Sylvia Ayres embarks on a two-year journey of discovery, not only about Midwifery, but about herself, as she blossoms from raw recruit to polished professional. The rose-tinted spectacles of perfect birth and motherhood are demolished on day one as she enters the world of clinical Midwifery, and the reader is taken on a rollercoaster of emotions during her first encounter of childbirth. Heart-warming normal births, catastrophic clinical emergencies, and humorous encounters are all recounted using the author's own clinical experiences and memories as a fledgling student Midwife in nineteen seventy-two in one of the busiest maternity units in the country.

Share her experiences that make her laugh out loud, cry with relief, or sink into the depths of despair. These are, she discovers, a daily part of what being a Midwife is all about. She is enamoured from day one, even though her first delivery experience is traumatic. The intimate nature of midwifery practice and the clinical and social problems of the women she meets throughout her training catapult her into situations where there is poverty, violence, and challenging relationships.

Working alongside her colleagues, Sylvia slowly unpicks the varied roles of staff that work within maternity services, from the legendary Mrs Annie O'Neil – senior Midwife tutor – to the labour ward cleaner, Mercy, provider of life-saving tea and toast! The complexity of Midwifery and obstetric problems are matched only by the many nuances of the lives and relationships within the families and mothers that she cares for. For two years her life is dominated by Midwifery textbooks, working shifts, day and night, and even having to live away from home for three months in a community house. She learns throughout her training not to be judgemental and marvells at the strength and endurance of the women she cares for. Follow in her footsteps and relive the experiences that changed her so profoundly and resulted in her feeling proud to call herself Midwife.

Sylvia in 1980

The 1972-Set

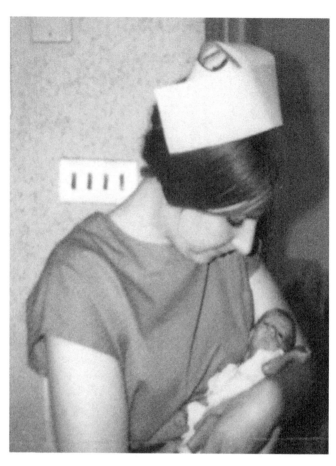

Working on the Special Care Baby Unit

Chapter One

Sylvia Ayres stood against the back wall of the room she was standing in and watched, mesmerised by what was taking place in front of her. Eight months ago, she had seen an advertisement in a local newspaper wanting applicants for Midwifery training. At the time she had been working as a nursery nurse in a variety of nursery schools and infant schools but, as much as she adored the babies and children, she still felt unfulfilled. She applied to the Midwifery training school, filled out and posted the required application forms, and was then asked to attend for an entrance examination and interview. She had broken the mould by first training as a Nursery Nurse, much to her mother's disquiet who was used to seeing an unbroken journey of school, then straight to work. To her utter amazement, two weeks later, a letter came through the letterbox informing her that she had been accepted for Midwifery training. Paperwork, references, and purchase of necessary reading requirements fulfilled, she was given a date on which she was to present herself. And three months later here she was, about to experience the biggest event of her twenty-one years. Even though she had never been inside the maternity unit before, she had history with the towering monolith, whose six floors could be seen for miles at night, lighting up the skyline. Sylvia's sister-in-law had been the first maternal death in the newly opened maternity unit four years previously, smothering the whole family with a cascade of crushing anguish and grief. Her first day would be bittersweet, tinged with sad memories but also with hopes of making a difference for other women. The local six-storey maternity unit covering a large geographical area was to be her place of training, and also a catharsis for what had passed before. Little did she know then that it would become almost her second home for the next forty years of her life.

That eventful morning had started badly. At six-fifteen she had left the warmth and security of her family home to catch two buses that would get her close to the hospital site. The bus that would take her on the last leg of her journey had chugged slowly through the snow-bound streets, the first snow of the year. Snow drifts had slowed city traffic almost to a halt and she needed to be at the hospital for seven o' clock to have time to get changed into the uniform that she had been measured up for. About to experience her first shift on the busy labour ward in one of the largest maternity hospitals in the country, she would soon know if she had made a mistake in choosing to enter the world of Midwifery.

Snow was coming down hard in great drifts, batted this way and that by a piercing wind. Sylvia was still trying to become familiar with bus routes and the best way to travel to the hospital complex and had asked the bus driver to put her off at the right stop. He forgot. It took another twenty minutes of walking back to get to where she needed to be after he had stopped the bus. She staggered through the main gates of the hospital grounds and reached the exterior of the six-storey building that dominated the skyline.

Reaching the side entrance of the hospital, she looked like a yeti in her full-length maxi coat with its huge fur collar covered in snow. Her platform sole boots in fake snakeskin might have been the bees' knees in terms of seventies fashion, but they were lethal to walk in in snow. She hadn't realised how far the walk from the bus stop to the grounds of the hospital was, and she was out of breath when she reached her destination, partly from exertion and partly from fear that she had bitten of more than she could chew by even thinking she was capable of training to be a professional.

She pushed open the large glass and metal double doors and stepped into a corridor located behind the side entrance doors. There were numerous uniformed individuals already walking purposely towards other large double doors on her left that led to another department. Strange noises and smells bombarded her senses, clanking trolleys, persistent background electronic bleeps, and a strong antiseptic smell that seemed to be everywhere. The background noise of electronic static and bleeps joined in the cacophony of a hospital department girding its loins for yet another busy day. As she continued walking down the corridor towards the stairs that led to the changing-rooms, a particularly smart-looking woman dressed in a navy-blue dress, a crisp white apron, and a frilly white cap walked past. She had a whole host of badges and name titles on her chest and exuded confidence and efficiency to such a degree that Sylvia was unnerved by it and a moment of sheer panic engulfed her. She mentally pulled herself together, took a deep breath, and carried on walking with a confidence that belied her inner apprehension.

She reached the lifts by the stairs that she knew took her down to the basement area, already thronged with large numbers of staff heading into a warren of underground corridors that ran the length and breadth of the hospital. Her uniform had been delivered to the basement changing-rooms in the maternity hospital a week ago and consisted of a number of mustard yellow dresses that she had been measured for and a whole pile of starched white aprons and caps. Most people associated student nurses and midwives with a blue uniform but direct-entry students who wished to train as midwives, with no previous training in nursing, had to wear yellow dresses. She was soon to discover that, to some, this was viewed as not having the same status as a State Registered Nurse who could complete a shorter length of Midwifery training because of previous experience, but that attitude had not yet made its mark on her outlook. Later she would learn from past experiences of other Midwives that direct-entry Midwives worked harder than ever to dispel the myth that they were inferior, and their promotion opportunities equalled their State Registered qualification colleagues on every level.

All of Sylvia's uniform dresses had her name printed onto the inside of the collar area so that, when they went to the hospital laundry, they would be returned to the changing-rooms in the basement corridor of the hospital. Her very favourite item was the full-length navy wool cape lined in red that fastened with criss-cross bands across her chest. It was warm and heavy, and she had been strangely comforted just by the act of putting it on, a bit like having a favourite snugly blanket that a child clung to for comfort.

The basement housed a coffee room, changing-rooms, and the porter's office. All soiled uniforms that were sent to the hospital's laundry department were transported via the basement. Staff could also collect freshly laundered uniforms from this area. Huge metal containers stood on the corridor and individually wrapped packs of uniforms could be found, freshly laundered and ready to be worn.

Sylvia joined the rest of her fellow students in the changing-rooms and experienced a rugby scrum of excited, chattering females in varying stages of undress, all coming to terms with the difficulties of trying to fold their starched caps and putting on spotless, white aprons that crackled as they were unfolded from the laundry wrapping. They too had been starched to within an inch of their lives. The noise was deafening as she hovered uncertainly by her locker, a grey metal affair in a line of many others. Realising time was getting on, she took off her coat, unlocked her locker, and unwrapped her uniform from its packing.

Half an hour later, wearing her uniform and an apron so starched it would have stood upright on the floor by itself, Sylvia found herself standing in a labour ward room that was accessed behind the large double doors off the corridor that she had so recently walked down. The area of the hospital where she now stood was known as the Labour Ward Suite and consisted of eight rooms and a theatre. It was the beating heart of the hospital and obstetric dramas of epic proportions regularly threw a series of frightening challenges to the stalwart staff who managed the six thousand plus deliveries every year. This huge workload was superseded by only one other hospital, in London, as the busiest maternity unit in the country. There was also an adjacent theatre and two or three rooms known as the Progress Department where women were admitted directly from home either in early labour or needing a diagnosis to match a bewildering array of clinical scenarios that all staff battled with twenty-four hours a day. To the uninitiated it could be very challenging, but it provided an excellent training ground for Midwives, students, and medical students alike.

Sylvia was supposed to be witnessing a normal

birth and her first day on the Labour Ward had started off in a very promising light. Sister Francis met her in the sitting-room on her arrival and informed her that there was a first-time mum, Natalie, well on in labour, and an ideal first birth to witness.

She was introduced to the mum and her husband by Sister Francis and then told to don a plastic apron and proceeded under instruction to wipe down with an antiseptic solution every available surface in the nearby empty labour rooms. Cleanliness was god, she soon discovered. Half an hour later Sister Francis had called her back into the room she was now standing in, as the lady's labour had progressed quickly and a delivery was expected soon.

The room was about twelve feet square, with most of one wall covered in opaque glass windows. It was one of four rooms down the left-hand side of the labour ward, and it was an area that she eventually would get to know very well indeed. There was a lot of equipment, noise, and people in such a small space and it was stiflingly hot, making Sylvia feel a little claustrophobic. She had positioned herself against the back wall, hoping not to be noticed, and was about to witness her first delivery, a memorable rite of passage for a fledgling student Midwife.

Shaking in her black regulation lace-up shoes and feeling sick, Sylvia nervously adjusted the unfamiliar starched apron that was wrapped around her small frame like a tight bed sheet. The cap was firmly attached to her head with most of a whole packet of hair grips. A tendril of hair had escaped from under her cap, and she pushed it back and surreptitiously wiped away the sweat that was already forming on her brow. Everyone in the room, including her, was wearing a paper mask and it felt scratchy and irritating against her face. The unfamiliar fob watch lay, as yet unused, pinned onto her chest next to her name badge, and she had a pocket full of biros, black and red, and a small notebook in her pocket. Heart pounding, she readjusted the paper mask that was threatening to suffocate her as she, along with other members of her intake, based in different departments in the hospital, prepared to experience their first taste of one of the oldest professions in the world.

Sylvia was not yet experienced enough to know which type of staff were wearing what uniforms and as there was such a variety of uniforms in the room, there were many she had no knowledge of. She knew that Sisters, senior clinicians, wore navy-blue dresses but that was the extent of her experience. It was incredibly hot in the room, and the temperature was also heightened by what looked like a heater that was situated over a baby changing mat that sat on top of a stainless-steel work trolley. It was connected to a load of machinery and equipment, plugged into the wall by the trolley. She shrank further back against the wall and tried to merge into the background.

In front of her, a very bright ceiling-mounted light attached to a moveable arm shone onto a stainless-steel bed that was surrounded by a number of staff.

On the bed was a woman, lying semi prone on her back, legs akimbo. A white nightdress rucked up around her waist, leaving the lower part of her torso exposed. A beam of light like a spotlight on a stage lit up the occupied bed in front of Sylvia. By the bed stood Sister Francis, her seniority denoted by the navy-blue uniform dress that she was wearing. She was encased in a green surgical gown and a mask that obscured the bottom half of her face. She too had sweat running down the side of her face, dripping off her eyebrows and onto the lenses of her glasses.

"Take these off," she ordered a nurse in a green uniform dress who was standing next to her. "Be careful not to touch, just the glasses," she instructed, ensuring, Sylvia found out later, her sterile status was not compromised. She watched from the back of the room as Sister Francis adjusted her stance, bent her knees and leaned forward, laying her left hand onto the woman's abdomen and gently inserting her second and third fingers of her right hand into the fleshy entrance to the woman's body. She was performing an examination that Sylvia would herself be performing many times during her training.

Watching, her initial response was to recoil from such an intimate examination in such a very public space. She knew, of course, that babies were born through the space that the midwife was examining so intently, and that she herself very shortly would be expected to perform such an examination with her support Midwife. Even so, it was an uneasy assault on her senses that she hadn't expected. She felt hugely excited, nervous, apprehensive, and a bit scared, all rolled up into one big emotional rollercoaster as she watched Sister Francis carry out the examination of her patient.

Chapter Two

Sister Francis had been caring for the patient in front of her for a number of hours now and she was concerned. She had been delivering babies for well over twenty-five years and her suspicions that all was not well were about to be confirmed. The space she was examining was impossibly tight and she knew from long years of experience that some extra help was going to be needed to facilitate the delivery of the baby.

Her fingertips sensitively probed inside the woman's birth canal, pushing further back into the fleshy cavity until she came into contact with what she was looking for. Gently she ran her fingers over the baby's skull and explored its surface to confirm what she had suspected.

Adjusting her weight and leaning forward slightly over the woman's torso, she probed further into the tight space, her fingertips pushing, gently seeking more information. Her suspicions of a deep transverse arrest were confirmed. The baby's head was well and truly stuck inside the bony structure that was the mother's pelvis, jammed tight against the bony framework. Without help there was no way this baby could be delivered vaginally.

"Call Mr Merton, call for medical aid now," she instructed her assistant. "Get the Paediatrician on call, inform the neonatal unit we may need a cot and get the Anaesthetist to come and top up this epidural."

Concentrated activity erupted in the room and Sylvia watched as various staff members carried out Sister Francis's instructions. She became more aware of an unfamiliar background noise that she suddenly realised had been there since she had entered the room. It was like a very fast heartbeat, continuous, insistent, like a train carving its journey down a track. It was the sound of a baby's heartbeat reverberating loudly in the room. It was coming from a machine attached to the mother's body.

Adjusting her already aching feet, Sylvia looked around the room and located the machine that was tucked right next to the bed where the mother lay. It was with this machine (called a foetal monitor) that the baby's heartbeat was being monitored with a pair of large flat metal discs that were strapped around the mother's abdomen with elastic straps. These were attached to the foetal monitor machine that was churning out masses of graph paper that had a printout of the baby's heartbeat and, she learned later, the mother's contractions. The sound of the baby's heartbeat echoed around the room and Sylvia could see that everyone's attention was on nothing else. Her ears locked into a sound that would eventually become a beautiful confirmation of life or an impending arbiter of disaster, but she was yet to reach that level of expertise.

The machines were a very new innovation, and prior to their arrival Midwives had listened to a baby's heartbeat before and during birth with a small, black plastic trumpet called a Pinards. It would be placed onto the mother's abdomen over where it was thought the baby's chest or back might be lying and the Midwife would place her ear over the other end and listen for and count the rate of baby's heartbeat. They were still used predominantly by Midwives, but the new monitors were used if there were expected problems with the labour or baby.

Sister Francis listened with mounting anxiety as the baby's heartbeat, echoing from all four walls of the room, accelerated to an unacceptable high, and then swooped down to a rate that scared her. The fast, train-like rhythm changed as the woman's contraction reached its height, and it slowed to a rate of barely one beat a second. The tracing on the monitor churned out the evidence that this baby was distressed and tiring fast. She didn't need to look at the graph paper and analyse its printout. She knew from what she was hearing. Foetal distress of this magnitude was any Midwife's nightmare and help was needed fast.

Sylvia could tell from the expressions on people's faces that something was very wrong, but she didn't know what. She watched with mounting anxiety as the room and its occupants exploded into activity, checking unknown equipment, applying an oxygen mask to the mother's face, drawing up drugs into syringes.

Sister Francis withdrew her hand gently from the mother's birth canal and stepped back. She approached the mother, who was lying on her back looking exhausted.

"Natalie, your baby is tired and so are you," she said gently, "we need to give you both some help."

She went on to explain that a forceps delivery was needed to help the baby out. This involved inserting specially shaped forceps called Kiellands that would help protect the baby's head, and also rotate it into a more favourable position for delivery.

She took off her blood-stained gloves and expertly threw them into a clinical waste bin at the bottom of the bed, continuing to shout out instructions as she did so to the other staff in the room.

Natalie was by now sweating profusely from the exertion of pushing, her white hospital gown still rucked up around her thighs. Her husband Jamie stood by her side, clutching her hand, looking white with exhaustion and worry. She was beginning to feel exhausted. She had had a few false labour pains in the days before labour proper had started and she had not slept well. She had been in labour for a number of hours with an epidural removing most of the discomfort, but being trapped on a bed and numb from the waist down was taking its toll.

Sister Francis was well-aware of the new student Midwife standing at the back of the room and she was fully aware of the vulnerability that she must have been feeling on her first shift. She had trained many students over the years, and she could see the anxiety in her eyes above the mask which covered most of Sylvia's face.

"Just come over here and give me a hand to put Natalie into lithotomy," she called to Sylvia. This involved putting the mother's heels into a supportive sling, one each side of the bed, enabling the obstetrician to take over and apply a set of forceps to the baby's head. Sylvia positioned herself on the left side of the steel-framed bed and tentatively watched what Sister Francis did. She picked up the mother's lower leg and guided her heel into the thick supportive strap that was then hooked onto an upright metal support at the side of the bed.

Because Natalie had an epidural, a tube inserted into the epidural space in her spinal cord, resulting in complete numbness from the waist down, she had no sensation of her lower limbs at all.

Sylvia found it quite difficult to control the movement of the mother's leg which felt very heavy and floppy, something she had not anticipated. Having to invade someone's personal space, let alone touch them in very personal parts of their body, was something that Sylvia had worried about when she had applied for training. Overcoming her reticence and taking a deep breath in, she grasped firmly Natalie's knee and thigh and managed to get her heel into the supportive leather strap. "There's not much dignity about having a baby," she thought as the arrival of the anaesthetist contributed to the filling of what seemed like a room already full of people.

The labour room door swung open yet again and Charles Merton, Consultant Obstetrician, made his entrance. This was his sixteenth straight hour on duty. He had been on call all of the previous night, where to date he had performed two emergency Caesarean sections, one breech extraction, sadly diagnosed an intra uterine death, and had carried out one manual removal of placenta, or afterbirth, that had formed an unhealthy attachment to its host. He had impeccable credentials, commanding a presence that had anyone within a few yards automatically gravitating towards him. He had charm by the bucketful, and he knew it.

He was also an experienced clinician of thirty years, on the hospital's board of governors and was an international speaker on how to manage obstetric emergencies as well as specialising in the management of a prolapsed cord, a serious obstetric emergency. He was well-liked by many of his colleagues, and he was one of the few consultants who joined in the social activities that Midwives frequently planned to keep themselves sane when the going got rough, which it did with an alarming regularity. Running a hand through his dishevelled silver-grey hair and suppressing a yawn he stepped quickly over to the locker at the side of the bed.

"OK, Sis, what have we got here then?" he said, as he picked up the mother's case notes and quickly scanned the records of the mother's labour. He introduced himself to both parents and Sister Francis filled him in on the progress, or lack of it, of the last hour. The situation was serious, an obstructed labour, an exhausted mother, and by the look of the foetal heart tracing, a baby that was seriously distressed and tiring fast.

Charles Merton listened with dismay to the decelerations of the baby's heartbeat. He lifted up the reams of paper that had been continuously recording the contractions and baby's heartbeat and scrutinised them intently. Immediate delivery now, it screamed at him. He'd seen this pattern before, and it scared him. He looked up at Sister Francis.

"Deep transverse arrest. Inform theatre it may be needed if there are difficulties," he said to a member of staff who left the room to call the theatre staff.

"We need to get your little one out as soon as possible," he explained to Natalie, as he started to scrub his hands at the nearby sink.

He was helped into a sterile, green, surgical gown, pulling on a pair of sterile gloves, all the time keeping his eyes and ears on the continually soaring and dipping of the baby's heartbeat, as more evidence of a baby who was literally dying in front of them was churned out of the machine next to Natalie's bed. Charles Merton knew it was going to be a close call getting the baby out alive and inwardly prayed he still had the stamina after sixteens hours on his feet to deal with it.

After explaining to Natalie that he needed to check the position of the baby, Charles applied a generous amount of a lubricating cream to his gloved hand and sensitively examined Natalie's birth canal, his probing fingers searching for a hard, bony head. There should have been an infant's head on the verge of making its entrance into the world. Instead, there was absolutely nothing low down in the genital tract, just lots of space with no pressure on the surrounding tissues, which, if baby's head was travelling down through the birth canal, as it should, there would be. He probed deeper into the very back of the woman's birth canal.

He noted that the cervix or neck of the womb was, indeed, fully dilated, and then he ran his fingers expertly over a hard, bony head, searching for the suture lines which allowed baby's head to mould for the journey through the mother's pelvis. As he thought, the position of the sagittal suture on baby's head confirmed what Sister Francis had found: a deep transverse arrest. This meant that the normal rotation of the baby's head as it travelled through the mother's pelvis had not occurred. The baby's head had tried to negotiate the pelvic space and become stuck deep inside the cavity. Sylvia could see Sister Francis preparing a trolley for a Kiellands rotation forceps delivery, opening sterile packs, checking equipment on the neonatal resuscitation unit, checking oxygen supplies, beginning to check with other staff members that the drugs that were going to be needed for this next procedure were being prepared for use.

Kiellands were a type of forceps with special attention being given to their structure. The two stainless-steel blades were curved and this would help the forceps to negotiate the dimensions and curves of the woman's pelvic outlet or birth canal. They were also constructed in this way to help protect the baby's head as they were clamped around the head to help delivery but to protect the delicate structures of a new-born's skull.

To Sylvia's eyes, they looked like instruments of torture. She watched the drama unfolding before her, her pulse rate beyond counting, and her mouth dry with anxiety. She had visions of fainting, making a fool of herself on her very first day, of not coping.

"I can do this," she thought fiercely.

"Nurse Ayres?" Sylvia didn't realise at first that it was she who was being addressed by Sister Francis.

"Go and support Natalie, will you? See if she needs anything."

Sylvia moved further up the side of the bed, where Natalie was lying, not sure of what she could do.

Tears were streaming down Natalie's face, but not through pain, as her topped up epidural was working wonderfully well. Exhaustion and the terror of hearing her baby's heartbeat racing like a train one minute, and then dropping like a stone the next confirmed her very worst suspicions.

For nine months she had carried inside, unsaid, the dread that her baby was going to die, that she would never take him home. Why, she didn't know. She had told no one of her fears, knew it was illogical, as she had had a very healthy pregnancy, but she just couldn't shake it off. She would awaken in the night, sweating, terror wrapped around her form like a second skin, holding her breath, and almost crying with relief when she felt the baby moving inside her. And here she was again, beginning to live the nightmare that had trailed her subconscious for most of her pregnancy.

Sylvia took hold of Natalie's hand, and almost immediately wished she hadn't as the vice-like grip crushed her fingers to burning point. Feeling utterly useless, Sylvia leaned forward and whispered,

"Come on, you are doing fine, it won't be long now," not knowing if that was true or not. She could see the terror in the mother's eyes and thought that the very least she could do was to offer some encouragement.

"Just listen to what the doctor and Sister Francis tell you, and you will be fine."

In the background she could hear Sister Francis asking Jamie, Natalie's husband, to wait outside in the waiting room that was in the Progress Department, and one of the staff escorted him away.

At the other end of the bed, Charles Merton was now sitting on a stool directly in front of the mother's body. The bottom half of the bed slid under the top half of the bed, allowing much closer access. His right hand was deeply embedded in the mother's body, his left hand on top of her abdomen, assessing the baby's position and confirming it with the information from his fingertips.

He removed his fingers and picked up a pair of surgical scissors. Swiftly and deftly, he inserted the leading edge into the entrance to the woman's body and made a precise cut through the skin and muscle layers, enlarging the space available for the baby's head. Next, he picked up the stainless-steel forceps that had been handed to him by Sister Francis. Out of the corner of his eye he could see the Paediatrician who had arrived earlier, checking the oxygen supply, drawing up drugs, and checking that the heater was on over the infant rescusitaire.

Taking hold of first one forceps, then another, he expertly slid them inside the mother's body. First one blade, fitting snugly around the baby's skull, then the next, locking the two blades of the forceps together, so he could start to rotate the baby's skull into a more favourable position.

"I want you to start pushing," he said to Natalie, who took a deep breathe in and pushed as if her life depended on it, which it did, because Natalie could not bear the thought of existence without her baby beside her. Slowly Charles Merton manoeuvred, adding downward traction as Natalie pushed, deep guttural sounds coming from her throat.

Sylvia's hand was still clamped in Natalie's vice-like grip, but not for all the tea in China could she or would she let go. She watched the incredible teamwork taking place in front of her and marvelled at the skill of everyone who knew exactly what they needed to do. Sister Francis had her hand on Natalie's abdomen, feeling for contractions, as Natalie's epidural stopped her from knowing when a contraction was occurring.

"Right, you've got another one coming, push," she instructed.

"Come on, Natalie you can do this."

Charles pulled down on the forceps, felt a sudden give of the resistance, and noticed with great relief that the baby's head was slowly appearing at the vulva, the entrance to the mother's body. He disengaged the forceps, removing them as expertly as he had applied them, and checked for any loops of cord around the baby's neck, which thankfully there wasn't. He placed both hands, one on each side of the baby's head, and applied more traction, down towards the delivery bed. As he did so, one of the baby's shoulders slid out from underneath the mother's pubic arch. He quickly reversed the manoeuvre and delivered the other shoulder. With one deft movement, he lifted the baby up, a boy, and laid him across his mother's abdomen.

Sylvia was unaware of the tears streaming down her face; only of the tears of Natalie. She breathed a huge sigh of relief, which was followed immediately by a cold dread, clamping itself around her chest like an iron fist. The baby was not moving.

He lay sprawled across his mother's abdomen, his trailing umbilical cord wrapped around his body. He made no sound, and his little limbs were limp and unmoving. His skin was not the pink, plump, healthy covering that Sylvia had seen in movies or television serials, this baby's skin was a pasty white with a bluish tinge. She noticed a strange green, brown substance smeared upon his body and around his neck. There was no tone in his little muscles, just a terrible floppiness, so noticeable as an assistant placed an oxygen mask over the baby's nose and mouth. Sister Francis swiftly cut and clamped the cord. She unwrapped it swiftly from around his body and took the baby over to the resuscitation unit where the Paediatrician was waiting for him.

"What's the matter, why isn't he crying?" said Natalie, echoing the same fears as Sylvia.

"He just needs a little help to get him breathing properly," said Sister Francis. She stood next to the Paediatrician who by now was busy sucking out a lethal mixture of amniotic fluid and meconium, a black-looking tarry substance that had been expelled, inside the womb, from the baby's bowels as he became more and more starved of oxygen. She knew that speed was of the essence, to get as much of the toxic mix out of his lungs as quickly as possible, if this baby was to stand any chance of breathing.

"Apgar at one minute, three," said Sister Francis to the assistant, who wrote this piece of information onto her pocket notepad.

The Paediatrician swiftly inserted a large steel instrument into the baby's mouth and Sister Francis handed him what looked like a very thin piece of plastic tubing with a tiny hole on one end, which he inserted into the metallic laryngoscope, firmly sited in the baby's mouth. He gently pushed the tube down, attaching the other end to an oxygen supply.

"Come on, baby," he whispered quietly, as life-giving oxygen started to pour into the tiny lungs. Natalie watched, and died a hundred deaths as the seconds of silence ticked by.

Sylvia was still clutching the mother's hand in a vice-like grip that would have done a navvy in an arm-wrestling competition proud.

"I'm not going to be strong enough for this," she thought. "I've made a big mistake," and tears started to form in the corner of her eyes. Natalie was now absolutely silent, as were all the staff in the room. Her worst fears were being realised, that dream throughout her pregnancy where she sat holding a lifeless baby was coming true.

Suddenly, there was a flicker in a tiny finger, a plump little leg twitched, the baby's chest started to move, erratic at first, then regularly as the oxygen did its work of reversing the crippling acidosis developing in the baby's blood stream. A seemingly miraculous pinky tinge began to suffuse the baby's body, and the paediatrician gently withdrew the plastic cannula, and the laryngoscope, as the baby let out a cry that was shocking in its intensity. An almost collective sigh of relief pervaded the room.

"Apgar seven at five minutes," said Sister Francis.

"Is he alright?" said Natalie.

"Look," he said gently, "you can see for yourselves, he's perfect."

Sylvia stood, transfixed, at the top end of the bed. The mother had to gently disengage her fingers so she could reach out and hold her baby as Sylvia was still gripping her hand tightly. Her tears of despair and fear had swiftly turned into tears of relief and joy. Sylvia felt overwhelmed. How could that huge, stretched abdomen in such a petite frame have harboured the miracle that was now bawling his little head of in his mother's arms?

Natalie was ecstatic as her baby, wrapped in a white towel, was placed in her arms. She pulled back the towel to reveal a face as perfect as a peach, eyes wide open and a pink rosebud mouth, all topped by a thatch of dark hair. In wonderment, she opened the towel a little more to reveal the round, supple limbs, and as she gently started to explore him with her hand, a tiny finger wrapped itself around one of hers, and hung on like a limpet. Two pairs of eyes locked in an endless moment of connection and the bonding had begun.

"Thank you," said the mother, simply and quietly as an assistant helped her to comfortably hold her baby.

Sylvia said, "No, thank you for letting me be here with you." Following Sister Francis's instructions, she walked out of the delivery room and around the corner to the waiting room, where Natalie's husband was pacing frantically, waiting for news, and she had the great pleasure of informing him that he had a son. He threw his arms around Sylvia, crushing her against his woolly jumper, saying 'thank you, thank you' in between exclamations of 'great! great!'

Meanwhile Charles Merton, still at the other end of Natalie's bed, was completing the delivery of the afterbirth, a large pink, fleshy mass about the size of a dinner plate that had kept baby alive and well inside the womb.

"All looks complete to me," he told Sister Francis, "but I know you will give it a thorough check."

He now needed to suture Natalie's perineum back together. The perineum was the area of skin and muscle layers that he had cut through to enable forceps to be inserted into the birth canal. It needed to be expertly sutured back together again so that Natalie's pelvic floor was fully functioning after her delivery. Natalie was completely unaware that this procedure had been carried out, as her epidural had been topped up by the anaesthetist just before delivery of her baby and the obstetrician, desperate to expedite delivery of a deeply distressed baby, had left the explanation until after the event.

As Sister Francis expertly dropped sterile suturing needles and catgut onto the delivery trolley, he explained to both parents why he had needed to carry out an episiotomy.

Sister Francis, writing furiously in the notes in an attempt to keep up to date with the minute-by-minute account of events, looked across the room to where Sylvia was standing. She recognised in the student midwife's expression only too well the sudden stillness and look of desperation.

She called Sylvia across the room to stand next to her as she wrote down in the mother's notes a very detailed account of all that had taken place in the delivery room, explaining some terminology as she did so. Sylvia was feeling overwhelmed. There had been no warning about the episiotomy, and to witness it had quite shocked her. She had heard about them and knew without a shadow of a doubt that this baby's life had been saved because one had been performed to quickly hasten the delivery. She felt sick and a bit faint.

Sister Francis, ever observant, had noticed. "Come with me, Nurse Ayres, I need to check this placenta and you can do it with me." She opened the labour room door and pushed the delivery trolley down the corridor and into the nearest sluice room. Sylvia followed, hastily wiping her face and hoping that Sister Francis had not seen her tears.

"Well, quite a start for your first day on the job," said Sister Francis. "We normally try and get you to witness a few normal deliveries first if we can, but of course you can't always dictate what the outcome's going to be."

She started to clear away the trolley, tipped paper packs into one bin, soiled bloodied swabs into another, and emptied a variety of small forceps, scissors, and clamps into a large sink for washing. These would later be sent to the sterilisation unit in the hospital grounds to be cleansed and then repacked into sealed sterilised delivery packs.

"It's all a bit overwhelming at first, isn't it?" she said kindly, giving Sylvia an opening to say how she felt. "I still clearly remember my very first day. I thought that I might as well go home as I would never be able to do the things I was witnessing, and hey, thirty-three years later, I'm still here."

Sylvia said, "I think I've made a mistake," and burst into a flood of tears.

Sister Francis quietly pushed the sluice door closed, giving them a little privacy, and waited patiently for the storm to abate.

"Here," she said, handing Sylvia a tissue. "We are going to check this placenta together, make sure mum and dad have a well-earned cup of tea and toast and then sort the rest of the notes out. As for having made a mistake, no, I don't think so, you demonstrated care and compassion to that mum whilst being under a lot of stress yourself, you put her feelings first, you gave her some loving touch, even though she nearly broke your hand in the process."

Sister Francis put the plastic dish holding the placenta into the sink and turned on the tap.

"And," she continued, "you do have two years, minus the last hour, to complete your training, so I reckon there's still time to turn you into a Midwife!"

The last was said with more than a twinkle in her eyes.

"Right, let's examine this placenta …"

Ten minutes later, with a mass of new clinical data about afterbirths and placentas swimming around in her head, Sylvia manoeuvred the now cleared trolley back to the delivery room.

She pushed the door open and saw that Natalie had on a clean nightgown, and that dad was holding his son, looking down at him, talking softly. The baby was staring at him, mesmerised by the sound of his voice. That moment was theirs, a new life, new hopes, and new beginnings. Sylvia thought it was one of the most moving things she had ever witnessed, and felt the tears starting to surface yet again.

"Get a grip Ayresie," she said to herself and, feeling a little surge of confidence, asked the Midwife if there was anything she could do to help.

Charles Merton had finished his record keeping of the baby he had just delivered and was sprawled in an armchair in the doctor's sitting-room which was situated at the entrance to the Labour Ward. He was drinking a cup of coffee, surrounded by a group of young housemen and very junior medical students who, as part of their training, were working alongside the obstetric staff on the Labour Ward suite. He was discussing with them the details of the forceps delivery he had just completed and he had a spellbound audience of junior staff who hung onto his every word. To them he represented the pinnacle of success. His star had risen, professionally, academically, and socially and his status was what they would spend most of their future careers trying to achieve.

But Mr Merton, as he was respectfully called, had a secret. If it got out it would destroy him, his career, and his marriage to a wife to whom status was everything.

He had a habit, a very bad one, and so far he had avoided detection. Fortunately for him, the hierarchy of his position had protected him from any noticeable scrutiny. Staff were only too pleased for a man in his senior role to help them out by administering occasional injections of the drug Pethidine to mothers on his case list who needed pain relief. These cases were always abnormal with high risks for mother and baby and the high activity and complex care needs made midwives grateful for the odd act of clinical support from the medical fraternity. Unfortunately, regardless of his meticulous record keeping, handwritten in the notes with the date and time the drug was administered, patients didn't get it, or at least only some of it – he did. Sometimes a woman who was near to delivery would be given just half an ampule of Pethidine, a pain-relieving injection. The other half would be discarded, or not, if it was Charles Merton who was drawing it up.

It was common practice for the Midwife in charge of a shift to routinely count up how many phials of Pethidine were in the box in the drugs cupboard and to meticulously record it. It was an easy matter to photocopy that sheet from time to time and add the name of a woman who had delivered within the last week. As long as the number of phials on the sheet tallied with the number of phials in the box of Pethidine, staff rarely, if ever, looked any further.

He knew which Midwives were lax in their record

keeping or who were delighted when he popped into a case they were caring for and he generously saved them the trip to the drugs cupboard. He dripped with charm when the occasion demanded it, and he could turn it off and on like a tap as they gave him the keys to the drugs cupboard. He had developed the Pethidine habit a few years ago, when he was going through a rocky patch with his wife and his career. Charming to staff and patients alike, his chemical need had so far been undetected. He was careful, he knew the risks.

The next few hours for Sylvia passed in a blur of information overload. Her feet ached, her back ached, and she never stopped moving, either to strip off used bed linen and wash down each bed with an antiseptic solution before remaking it again or to be clearing off trollies that had been used in other delivery rooms for a variety of procedures. She started to become aware of the layout of the rooms, what was stored in the many storage areas and, crucially where the kitchen was that supplied regular tea and toast to mums, dads, and staff either before, during, or after birth.

The cleaner who had responsibility for the kitchen

was Mercy whose bark was worse than her bite. Rake thin, sallow complexion, and dark brown, frizzy, home-dyed hair, she had a permanent appendage of a dishcloth and a tea towel in her hands and wore the hospital supplied green, wrap-around overall that all cleaning staff wore. Mercy's idea of a good cup of tea was that it needed to be so strong you could almost stand a teaspoon up in it. Someone once said, "the quality of Mercy is not strained, and neither is her tea" but it was said with great affection for a member of the labour ward staff whose job title had the least qualifications but whose timely supply of hot tea and toast was as welcome as the Consultant was for an emergency Caesarean section case. When working she was the dominatrix of her kitchen, and all staff knew it. For all her seeming impatience at the never-ending stream of dirty cups, plates, used tea trays that littered the work surface of her domain, and a toaster that was never out of use, she had a heart of gold, especially for the young students who frequently missed lunch breaks. They would thankfully, six hours into a shift and with no possibility of a lunch break, accept a well-earned cup of tea and a slice of toast from Mercy, often gulped down and eaten standing in a corner of her tiny kitchenette which was situated between the theatre and progress department. At first,

Sylvia was a bit scared of Mercy who had a blunt, some saw as intimidating, way of talking back at you, and not with you. But she would find later a softer heart behind the dominant persona and over time grow to like her.

Three hours later, with aching feet, and hands she had washed so many times she had lost count, Sylvia met Rosie Smith, her friend and fellow trainee, down in the basement coffee room where they had precisely twenty minutes (and no more, mind!) to collapse into old, battered armchairs that had been donated years previously by a grateful patient. Having grabbed a coffee from the counter, Sylvia looked across the room and saw a number of faces that she recognised from the exam and interview day, most looking animated and exhilarated. The noise level was deafening as students fiddled with their newly starched caps and spotlessly white aprons, swapping experiences of their first shift as student midwives in one of the busiest units in the country. Rosie had been on an antenatal ward and was already being instructed on how to give an injection and to test urine samples. Sylvia had so much she wanted to tell Rosie, and they swapped details of their first morning's work.

Twenty minutes flew by, and Sylvia heaved herself out of the comfortable armchair and climbed the stairs from the basement, back up to the Labour Ward. It seemed busier than ever as she manoeuvred past a mounting line of trollies in the Labour Ward corridor.

On return, she was instructed to go into labour room six, where she was to receive some information about sterile technique, whatever that was. She pushed open the door and found that another four students were also inside, lined up against a wall, looking as if they were about to be shot, which unknown to them, verbally, they were.

Sister Frenchit, who was to instruct them, was tiny in stature but her caustic wit and loud voice more than made up for any lack of physical build. She had white hair styled in a never changing tight perm. She had sharp features to go with her sharp repartee and wore metal-rimmed glasses over those piercing blue eyes that peered over with a searchlight intensity. She ran her high-risk antenatal ward with a rod of iron and was infamous for making sarcastic comments if any student or member of staff did not abide by her rules. She did not suffer fools at any price, always expected no less than perfection, and came down very heavily on anyone who did not act in a supremely professional manner on her ward. Rumour had it that she had been involved in some traumatic clinical disaster resulting in the death of a patient and that was why she was so pedantic in her insistence of scrupulous attention to procedure. Tales about her were legendary and the medical staff were not exempt from her rod-of-iron management of the antenatal high-risk department. On one noteworthy occasion, she had ejected a newly arrived houseman from her ward one night when he had arrived wearing green theatre scrubs, of which the trousers were too big and the only thing he could find to hold them up as he changed in theatre was some plastic string that had adorned the side of a large box of sterile gloves! She had in no uncertain terms demanded that he go and get dressed properly and not come back until he had, and he had meekly complied, much to the amusement of the staff who were present.

Sylvia went and stood at the end of the row of students and waited with a little apprehension for the onslaught of yet another new experience.

"Today," said Sister Frenchit, walking up and down the row of nervous students like a sergeant major on inspection parade, "I am going to show you how to wash your hands and put on a pair of gloves."

There was silence, and then a few suppressed sniggers and grins from some of the other students.

"God," said someone in a whisper, "she'll be showing us how to blow our noses next."

The unfortunate owner of this response was Penny Jones. There had been some concerns about her during the selection process for training, but the panel of selectors felt that she fulfilled the criteria for entry and that her very rough edges and seeming inability to listen and shut up at the right moments would be smoothed out during her training. Sister Frenchit's eagle eye and almost supernatural hearing picked up on the culprit immediately.

"You, your name?" barked Sister Frenchit.

"Penny Jones, Sister," said Penny, now wishing fervently that the ground would open up and swallow her.

"You do not speak until spoken to, or I ask you to answer a question, is that very clearly understood?"

All eyes were on Penny who by this time had turned a startling shade of red.

"OK, Sis," said Penny. This response produced a distinctly dire effect upon Sister Frenchit who by now looked as if she was going to explode. Sister Frenchit's piercing blue eyes bored into Penny's as she visibly drew in a deep breath to calm herself before the offending student.

"Do not use the word 'OK', it is slang, unprofessional, and not acceptable under any circumstances. My name is Sister Frenchit, no more, no less, and I expect you to use my full title with no abbreviations at any time. Is that clear?"

She addressed the last few words to the whole of the group, who in unison, reminiscent of primary school responses, said,

"Yes, Sister Frenchit."

Sylvia moved to the back of the group, trying not to be noticed, as Sister Frenchit demonstrated how they must master the technique of washing their hands, using a precise formula of movement. During the process each individual finger, and parts of the front and backs of the hands and wrists, were to be washed using wall-mounted Hibbiscrub, a powerful antiseptic wash solution. Following this, each student was then shown how to open a pack of sterile rubber gloves and put them on without de-sterilising the outside of the gloves. All of the students were instructed to perform the manoeuvre at least twice, and if the procedure was not satisfactory then they were informed that they would not be leaving the room until it was.

Sylvia was successful after three attempts, but Penny was the last to succeed, and finally after five attempts got it right. Putting on a pair of sterile gloves without decontaminating the outside with your technically 'dirty' hands, even though they had been washed and scrubbed within an inch of their life, was not an easy thing to achieve. Once again, there was a logical technique starting with how one opened the packet of sterile gloves, and all the group needed at least three attempts to get it right. Sister Frenchit's eagle eyes watched as they valiantly tried to touch only the inside of the glove with their washed hands, trying to slide their fingers inside and touching nothing else at all. Even the tiniest slip-up resulted in yet another pair of gloves being thrown into the bin with a terse 'do it again' ringing in their ears.

Finally, Sister Frenchit informed them that they were competent.

When she had left the room, Sylvia and Penny breathed a deep sigh of relief, echoed by the rest of the group.

"Blimey," said Penny, "I'll never open my mouth again."

Sylvia was still reeling from information overload about sterile technique procedures being the foundation of all nursing and midwifery clinical care, and the fact that her named midwife, her mentor, would be wanting to witness what they had just practised so that she would be able to sign Sylvia off as competent in that procedure, one of hundreds that would dominate her life as a student midwife for the next two years.

She left the room she was in and walked around to the other side of the labour ward, passing more rooms full of labouring women and staff scurrying up and down the corridors in a ceaseless flurry of movement She sought out Sister Francis and enquired about the baby now called James, whose birth she had witnessed that morning.

"He's gone to Special Care Baby Unit," said Sister Francis. "Just overnight so they can observe him. He swallowed quite a lot of meconium during delivery and even though it was successfully sucked out, there may be some residue left inside. If you pop along and explain who you are, they may let you in to check on him."

The neonatal unit was down the end of a long corridor next to the progress department. Sylvia buzzed the locked doors which were full of posters about instructions to visitors and staff to use the hand antiseptic solution positioned on the wall to the left of the doors before they entered, and surprised herself as she began to emulate the procedures she had spent half the afternoon practising, rubbing the solution up and down each finger, even around each nail bed. A voice on the intercom on the wall enquired who she was, and after a brief explanation, the doors gave an audible click and swung open, allowing her access to a ward area that was crammed full with some of the most technical, advanced, lifesaving equipment available to neonates.

As she walked through the corridor to the nurse station, she could see into each room she passed. They were full of banks of machinery, blinking lights, beeping monitors, strange whooshing noises, almost like sighs and in the middle of this mountain of technology, the tiniest bodies she had ever seen in her life, lying like little stranded beached life forms inside large plastic boxes. She couldn't tear her eyes away, as she saw a little baby, smaller, she would swear later, than her own battered teddy from childhood, attached to so many tubes and drips that she lost count.

"Can I help?" said a voice from behind. Sylvia turned to see the manager of the Special Care Baby Unit.

She explained who she was and why she had come and was escorted into a room that had one occupied incubator. Baby James looked impossibly large compared to the other babies on the ward, as he lay naked, for improved observation access from the neonatal nurses looking after him. He was to be observed for at least twenty-four hours to make sure no infections developed within his lungs, following his traumatic start in life.

The baby yawned, screwed up his face in a comical grimace, stretched, and opened his eyes. He stared at Sylvia's face and held her gaze, and that was how the room's co-ordinator found them ten minutes later.

"You'll need to go now, I need to do a few observation checks on him, but you can pop in tomorrow if you want to."

Sylvia smiled her thanks and walked out back to the Labour Ward where Sister Francis was waiting for her. She explained to Sylvia that they were going to examine a lady's abdomen so that she could learn how to define precisely and accurately in what position a baby was lying inside the mother's uterus, and there was a mother who had no objections to being examined by a student. Sylvia followed Sister Francis into labour room one and washed her hands as Sister Francis introduced Sylvia and explained what they were going to do.

The procedure that Sister Francis introduced to Sylvia demonstrated a crucial skill, the foundation of caring for a woman during pregnancy and labour and was called an abdominal palpation. It had to be mastered early on and honed to a great level of accuracy. The main aim of it was to accurately define exactly what position the baby inside the womb was lying in relation to the mother's pelvis. Lots of related information needed to be assessed at the same time, including the size of the baby, was it growing as it should, how far down into the mother's pelvis had the presenting part (usually baby's head, but not always) descended …

The examination was completed after using a pinards (this looking like a small, black, plastic trumpet) to locate and listen to the baby's heartbeat, which was counted for a full minute. Many important decisions during care pregnancy and labour were made following the finds of an abdominal palpation.

There was a very defined set of manoeuvres in a set order that Sister Francis explained to Sylvia over the next twenty minutes as, under her expert guidance, she attempted to understand what she was being told and to apply it to the very pregnant abdomen that was in front of her. The mother was used to having new student Midwives examine her during labour, as this was her fifth child. She was relaxed, cheerful, and confident and chatted to Sylvia as if she had known her all of her life, which helped Sylvia feel not so nervous.

She stood on the right side of the mum in front of her and placed her hands onto the lady's abdomen and listened to Sister Francis's instructions. It was not expected that she would at this stage of her training be anywhere near proficient and Sister Francis was pleased when she could discern the broad expanse of baby's back and roughly show where she thought she could feel the hard round mass that was baby's head. Finding and listening to the baby's heartbeat was much trickier and Sister Francis explained that over time Sylvia's ear would eventually become much more attuned to the foetal heart beats and adjust accordingly. It was enough to actually hear it at this early stage of her training. The accurate counting and assessment of its rate and rhythm that resulted in life-or-death decisions would come later. Sylvia had been provided with a register where she was to document a minimum of fifty abdominal palpations that she had assessed correctly and which had been verified by a qualified Midwife. She had to document this evidence, written down using the same examination procedure for every one so that it became second nature to perform and record the whole process, helping it to become deeply embedded in her knowledge base.

Having completed her abdominal palpation register, Sister Francis said that Sylvia could go home as her shift was coming to an end. She went down to the basement changing-room and changed out of her uniform. It was crowded with other students all doing the same thing, chatting excitedly and swapping stories. She took off her cap and unpinned her now creased, less-than-pristine starched apron, which would be deposited in a laundry skip by the door. She stepped out of her yellow dress and hung it up inside her locker, thinking about all the experiences that had assaulted her senses throughout the day. Putting her own clothes on, she grabbed her coat and bag and made her way out of the changing-room.

She walked up the steps to the ground floor, past the lifts, into main reception, and through the hospital's main entrance, hugging the experiences and memories of that very special day around her. She smiled and knew she had made the right decision. She would be back tomorrow, and the next day, and for the rest of her working life.

Chapter Three

An alarm clock was ringing very loudly somewhere, and Sylvia turned over, placing her outstretched arm over her face and ears in an attempt to escape its noise. It didn't work and the noise didn't stop. She flung the covers back just as her mother opened her bedroom door and informed her that she was going to be very late for her shift if she didn't get a move on. Wearily she located the offending timepiece, turned off the alarm, and staggered into the shower next door. The cascading water jets revived her, and she began to think through the day that lay ahead. Six weeks had passed since she had started her training, six weeks of hectic shifts, few coffee breaks, even fewer lunch breaks, and feet that ached incessantly. She wouldn't have missed one second of it, and this amazed her mother who had never seen her daughter so animated about anything in her life. Her hand ached as much as her feet did due to the incessant note taking and writing up in detail of every lecture she attended, and there was a lot. Regardless of frequently feeling overwhelmed by the amount of theory that had to be learned, her enjoyment of the whole experience superseded any panic attacks about her own abilities.

She had witnessed quite a few normal deliveries now and understood that the only thing normal about each was that the babies came out headfirst. Unless, of course, they were a breech presentation, when they came out bottom first. All the other details, observations, and behaviours of the individual mothers were as unique as they were. She learned much about couples' relationships with each other when one of them was pain-wracked with childbirth; about how they related to, supported, or worked together as a team, or not, at one of the most significant parts of their relationships. She was endlessly staggered by the emotional turmoil that she felt when she watched that new life, seconds ago impossibly squeezed inside a body, emerging into the world. Tiny babies, all different, all waiting to be imprinted upon by life's chances. A little nugget of confidence was beginning to grow inside her. She no longer nervously stood back hoping not to be noticed, but willingly stepped forward to support mums in their delivery positions, which, she discovered, were as varied as the patterns on their nightgowns.

Midwifery was a very hands-on, practical profession and Sylvia had now been taught how to take blood pressures, temperatures, and pulses, and to test urine samples. Sister Francis was very pleased with her, she had been told by her tutor, which pleased Sylvia immensely.

She stepped out of the shower, dried, and dressed in super-fast time, and, chomping on a piece of toast, drove to the maternity unit in her bright red Mini. Her parents had seen how long the two bus rides and walk each way to get to the hospital site took her and they had managed to scrape together enough money for a second-hand Mini. She silently thanked her father who, the previous year, had insisted she take driving lessons, even though she didn't own a car. She had cried when they surprised her with it, and, knowing how difficult getting that money together would have been for them, made her even more determined than ever to complete her training.

Walking through the main entrance to the maternity hospital, past the main reception desk, past the lifts and downstairs to the basement, Sylvia was beginning to recognise the layout of the hospital and other staff. There were the porters and the cleaning ladies attached to each ward or department who reported directly to the Sister in charge of the ward There were nursery nurses, junior doctors, senior Registrars, and X-ray and phlebotomy service staff who ran the service for taking hundreds of blood tests daily.

The changing-rooms in the basement were a ferment of activity every day as students fought in the narrow space to don their uniforms, aprons, and stiff, starched caps. Putting on her uniform resulted in Sylvia becoming someone else as the starched aprons and caps transformed her mind-set. It helped to transport her into a work frame of mind and to channel her concentration and she marvelled that it did so.

Today was a day she felt very nervous about. Sylvia and some of the other students were going into theatre to witness a Caesarean section, and she was feeling apprehensive. It wasn't about seeing blood, as God knows she had seen so much of it in the last few weeks. She had witnessed more deliveries, helped to take care of pregnant women who were bleeding, recently delivered women who were bleeding, and worst of all and the scariest, a woman who had a blood-clotting disorder whose blood loss did not want to stop leaking from her body no matter what they did. It was very touch and go from what she gathered, but finally the highly skilled obstetric team who cared for her managed to control it. Her tutors had told them that they would later on in their training be learning about Disseminated Intravascular Coagulation and blood-clotting disorders which was what the lady was suffering from. No, it wasn't about seeing blood, it was about seeing that first incision in the skin, that deliberate action of cutting someone's body open that really troubled and scared her. She had, of course, seen midwives performing episiotomies, where a small cut is made into the perineum, an area of skin between the vaginal entrance and anus, helping to make the exit for baby's head a bit bigger, or if it looked like baby or mum was tiring, or too much pressure was going to cause extensive tissue trauma. This procedure carried out seconds before delivery did not now traumatise her but for some reason unknown to her, the thought of scalpels cutting into abdomens did.

As she walked down the corridor towards the labour ward suite, she could see that the theatre lights were on and that there was frantic activity just inside the entrance, where the theatre porters and midwives were manoeuvring a trolley through the doors towards the small room off the main theatre space. A very still form lay on the trolley, and Sylvia could see, even at that distance, how pale and waxen the mother's pallor was.

"What's going on?" This was directed towards Fred the porter who was holding the theatre doors open as the trolley disappeared from sight into the theatre admissions room.

At the same time Sylvia spied her friend, Penny, down the corridor, coming towards her, holding a large plastic bag full of the patient's belongings. She looked visibly upset, and anxiously peered through the theatre doors as she approached. "What's going on, Fred?" said Sylvia.

"I don't know, only just come on duty, and the lads in theatre should have gone home by now, but they needed all hands on deck to get this lady into theatre pronto."

Penny saw Sylvia and breathed a sigh of relief.

"Are you in theatre today? Can you give them these? They belong to the lady in there," she said, pointing into the theatre doors. The corridor was not the place to ask any further questions, as Sister Francis came around the corner, gently leading a young man by his arm towards the visitors' waiting area. She saw Sylvia and caught her eye in silent communication.

"Just go and make this young man a cup of tea, will you, and then we can bring his lovely son to him for a cuddle from his daddy."

Sylvia became aware of some very strong undercurrents, of Sister Francis's eyes compelling her not to ask anything more at that point. She did as she was instructed and returned with a hot mug of tea.

The young man was sitting with his head in his hands, weariness etched into his posture. He lifted up a face that was lined with worry, two days' worth of stubble and eyes that were struggling to stay open.

"Ah, bless you," he said as she placed the mug into his hands, which by now had a slight tremor.

The words poured out of him, and Sylvia recognised how traumatised and shocked he was. He couldn't quite comprehend how something so perfect and beautiful, the delivery of their long-awaited son, could end up in just a few minutes with his wife fighting for her life in a theatre just twelve feet away. "Don't worry," said Sylvia. "The staff here are brilliant and I'm sure your wife is having the very best of care. Drink your tea and I'll bring your baby round so you can give him a cuddle while your wife is in theatre."

"The afterbirth's stuck," he said. "It started to come out in pieces and she started to bleed and it wouldn't stop, and it all happened so fast, and I don't know what to do, and I want to be with her."

Trying to stay calm Sylvia reassured him once more, silently praying that she was right, and then she walked briskly back to the labour ward, towards room five, where a new-born baby was missing that crucial skin-to-skin contact with his mother. She walked towards the cot as Sister Francis reappeared, clutching a set of notes.

"Retained placenta, partial separation only and the uterus could not contract, so she started to bleed, big style."

"What will they do?"

"Anaesthetise her and manually try to peel the placenta off the inside of the uterus. Her blood loss is great so they will be manually squeezing some units of blood into her very quickly, and helping the uterus to contact strongly to control the haemorrhage by giving her some powerful drugs that will also help.

"It's a big obstetric emergency, and a little later I will go through the case with you in a lot more detail. This scenario often comes up in your written examination paper, so you will really need to know definitions, diagnosis, treatment, complications, and possible outcomes." Sylvia began to understand the reason for the frantic activity outside the theatre doors, and the enormity of the responsibility sitting on every member of staff's shoulders as they all pulled together as a team to save the life of a young mother.

"Go and make that dad feel a bit better, take him his lovely son, give him something good to think about for a little while," said Sister Frances, and she ushered Sylvia into a labour room where a Perspex cot stood rather forlornly, its occupant very quiet. She walked over and gently pulled the blankets back. As she did so a tiny, pink finger curled around her own and held on tight.

"Yes, that's right," whispered Sylvia, "you hold on, it's alright." She found herself increasingly doing this, talking all the time to new-borns, holding them very close, and whispering gently into their little shell-like ears. Her fellow students gently ribbed her and had already dubbed her the 'baby whisperer', but she didn't care.

Sylvia pushed the Perspex cot on wheels down the labour ward corridor, checking first that the baby was well and truly swaddled and warm. She could just see two pairs of very dark eyes and a little thatch of wispy hair peeking out of the blankets.

She pushed the cot through the doors of the visitors' waiting room to find the baby's father sitting where she had left him, tea untouched. He looked up as she walked towards him, his face grey with fatigue.

"I've a young man here that needs a cuddle from his daddy," she said.

She peeled back the blankets and picked up the baby, placing him into his dad's arms.

"That's it, support his head with your arm and hold him close, over your heart, it makes him feel safe," she explained. "And talk to him, he'll like that."

Dad, who Sylvia had discovered was called Jim, looked as if he was holding the world's most fragile piece of glass. He stood up gingerly and started to rock his little son in his arms.

"That's it, you're a natural," said Sylvia as Jim adjusted his stance and lifted his baby a little closer to his face. Two pairs of eyes scrutinised each other, two new universes opened and collided. Sylvia was gratified to see Jim's face begin to soften and relax, and a small smile ghosted briefly across his face. She was beginning to recognise a pattern to those first bonding moments between parents and their new-born. She had seen it happen quite a few times now, but also recognised that the time frame was very individual with each birth.

First, she noticed, parents would be tentative about touching their baby, their first contact usually through blankets and sheets. Then, with growing confidence, mothers would pull the towel or blankets open a little more and start to explore with their fingertips, tracing across a peachy skin, a rosebud mouth, touching the hands and feet, checking again the sex of their baby. Finally, they would become bolder, opening the towel or blanket more, and using the palm of the hand to explore the contours of their baby. She was beginning to understand the importance of touch on the bonding process and had been saddened and worried when one of the women, whose delivery she had witnessed in the past few weeks, had not wanted to touch her baby, a situation she found distressing and extremely worrying.

The baby's tiny pink hand was visible now and as dad's hand curled around it, the baby grasped a finger and clung on tight.

"Do you know what's happening with my wife?" asked Jim. "Is there any news?"

"Sit yourself down over here and I'll go and find out," said Sylvia, immediately regretting saying it, as if the news was not good she wasn't sure how she would handle it.

She walked back to the theatre doors, which by

now were firmly closed. There was a small side door entrance, which was the non-sterile entrance that staff used to first gain access to the theatre. She had learned that there were very strict rules and procedures that governed routines and actions of anyone setting foot into the 'sterile' areas of the theatre. Clothing and footwear had to be exchanged for green theatre scrubs and white clogs or shoes that were only worn in that particular space and wearing clothing that consisted of loose trousers and tunics in varying sizes. There were showers and toilets and lockers for the more permanent theatre staff. Once staff had put on their theatre garb, the next step was to walk through into the scrubbing-up area, which was in the theatre itself. Here was a long run of stainless-steel sinks and taps, set in a shower-like setting, where sterile procedures reigned supreme. Hands were thoroughly scrubbed using the technique that Sylvia had witnessed on her first day. She had become quite competent at it now, as she had spent every day on duty having to carry out that procedure at least a dozen times a day.

As she wasn't 'sterile' and could see no one in the changing-room, she tentatively pushed open the connecting door into the scrubbing up area and peered round.

Beryl, the healthcare assistant, was manoeuvring great stainless-steel trays of instruments into the autoclave, a massive stainless-steel sterilising unit. Sylvia had decided she would never master the names of those instruments when two weeks previously the midwifery tutor had given them a brief tour of the theatre and had explained what some of the instruments were for and what they were called. Green armitage clamps and toothed and non-toothed forceps came to mind, as she had looked at what seemed an impossible number of instruments that might be used for just one Caesarean section.

"Are you ok, love, can I help you?" said Beryl.

All the students loved Beryl who had a cheery disposition, was approachable, and of whom they could ask about anything and not be made to feel stupid, which was more than could be said for some others she could mention.

"The dad wants to know what's happening. He's up in the visitors' waiting room with his baby," explained Sylvia.

"I'll get hold of the theatre Sister to have a word with you," said Beryl, continuing to check and rearrange instruments like she was setting a table, but with military precision. Sylvia retreated into the changing area and took a seat while she waited for further news and in a short while the door swung open and in came Frankie Lyons, peeling off her theatre cap that covered an unruly head of red curls, and pulling a paper mask away from her mouth and nose.

"That was a close call, don't want another one of those before breakfast, I can tell you," she said. She breathed a sigh of relief and informed Sylvia that the placenta was out, the bleeding controlled, and that the mother was in a stable condition.

"She's lost quite a lot of blood and we're transfusing her now; she will be going back to the labour ward for a while so she can be carefully monitored for a few hours. Do you want to go and bring dad to the theatre doors, with baby, so he can see his wife for a few moments, say in about thirty minutes or so?"

Sylvia nodded, thanked her, and went back to the visitors' waiting area, where she was pleased to see dad still gazing with rapt attention into his son's face. He visibly relaxed when she told him the good news, and she saw tears start to form in his eyes as he worked the muscles of his face to try and control any other outward show of emotion.

"I'll be back in about half an hour to take you see

your wife. Now, would you like some toast and more tea to keep you going?"

Jim nodded his thanks and Sylvia walked back down the corridor to the kitchenette, where there was a permanent, twenty-four-seven supply of tea and toast. She mused on the restorative qualities of such simple fair as she poured boiling water out of the geyser onto the teabag in the mug and put some bread into the toaster. Most of the staff, Consultants included, were beholden to the restorative qualities of tea and toast. Coffee breaks were often missed, and so were lunch breaks, with a daily regularity that made snatching a quick brew a necessity if you were to be able to stay upright, lifting, pushing, manoeuvring, and supporting bodies in an endless variety of situations for at least eight hours, often longer. No one was going to go home at the appointed hour of shift end if a baby you had monitored continually for eight hours was just ready to make his or her entrance. Brief snatches of conversations with fellow students, tit-bits of gossip, and worries and fears were exchanged at this communal watering-hole for staff. Here, young medical students, who were as nervous and inexperienced as Sylvia, would discuss shift notes and medical seminars, standing out as new boys in their crisp, white coats and yet-to-be-used stethoscopes, which were worn like a badge of pride around their necks.

Toast and tea sorted, Sylvia returned to the waiting area, deposited the life-saving supplies to Jim, and then went to find Sister Francis, who was by this time standing in the corridor talking to Penny Jones, whose face was beetroot red. Sylvia's heart sank at the sight of her friend's discomfort, as it was obvious that Penny was receiving a severe reprimand from Sister Francis.

"The next section is scheduled in about one hour's time. I want you both to go in and observe it, and then write it up in your deliveries book. After that you can go to lunch," said Sister Francis. "And, Nurse Jones, remember what I said!" and with that she walked briskly back to the nurse station area to study a whiteboard that had every room clearly marked with the details of who was in it, diagnosis, and details of staff responsible for that case. She was the labour ward co-ordinator for that shift; a huge responsibility that only very experienced clinicians took part in.

"What was that all about?" whispered Sylvia to her friend.

Penny's colour had receded a little and she raised her eyes to the ceiling, saying, "Disasters just seem to follow me around. I drop things, de-sterilise things without meaning to, and I forgot to label a twenty-four hour urine sample properly which resulted in the whole lot, a demijohn full of the stuff, having to be thrown away! And she doesn't even know about the most embarrassing thing yet, but I'm sure she will find out. I was mortified!" said Penny.

"What do you mean, embarrassing, what have you done?" said Sylvia.

"Not me, her!" hissed Penny as Sister Debbie Mathews, a tall, immaculately groomed midwife wearing the biggest set of long false eyelashes ever seen sashayed past, her navy-blue uniform looking like the only one in the building that had been created by a top fashion designer as it clung to her shapely form.

"What do you mean?" whispered Sylvia, who looked on as every pair of male eyes in the corridor space followed Debbie Mathews' retreating form.

"I caught them at it in the shower room, by the downstairs changing-room when I went to get a spare pen out of my locker," said Penny.

"What? Who was she with?" said Sylvia, agog with excitement at this juicy bit of gossip.

"Mr Charles Ash himself, would you believe?" said Penny. "I was that embarrassed I just stood there like a fish with my mouth open as they both tried to adjust their clothing and then he tripped up and fell over and her bleep went off with someone requesting back-up for a delivery that was about to take place in the back of a car in a lay-by. I looked at them both, him on the floor, and thought about the word 'lay-by', and that was it, it creased me and I started to laugh, which was not the thing to do but I just couldn't help myself."

By this time tears were streaming down Sylvia's face as she tried to remain in control, listening to her friend's account and finding it difficult to imagine the very starchy, unapproachable Consultant Anaesthetist Mr Charles Ash in a state of dishevelment with Debbie Mathews.

"Unfortunately, they were by this time standing up in the corner by my locker and I asked if they could move as I needed a pen, at which point Charles Ash muttered some very unrepeatable phrases and almost threw his own pen at me. I decided this was the time for me to beat a hasty retreat and left them to it!"

Sylvia had heard tit-bits of gossip about Debbie Mathews but thought they were all exaggerated. Obviously not!

"I'll meet you for lunch," said Sylvia, "and you can

fill me in on the rest." At this, they parted, Penny to find another large urine collection jar and Sylvia to take Jim to see his wife, who was now conscious and asking to see her husband and child.

Chapter Four

The small theatre changing-room was crowded as the female staff struggled in the confined space to don their theatre garb. A similar scenario was taking place a few feet away in the male changing-room as Consultant Obstetrician Richard Toft, Anaesthetist Mr Charles Ash, and Junior House Officer David Mellor pulled on their theatre uniforms and headed to the scrub-up area of the theatre. Sylvia was standing on one leg, pushing her foot into a pair of white theatre wellington boots, which were one size too big. They were the only pair left after the rugby scrum of trying to find trousers and a tunic top that vaguely fitted her. She hadn't shared her fears about viewing a Caesarean section with anyone, not even her mum, and she could feel her pulse pounding, her mouth dry, her stomach churning, silently praying she wouldn't make a fool of herself. She followed the others through the door into the scrub-up area where she was greeted by the reassuring sound of friendly banter over the top of cascading tap water as every station was fully occupied by staff using a special medicated scrub to clean hands and arms up to the elbow with individual small brushes. She took her place, finding a bit of confidence in the fact that she could adequately scrub-up almost on autopilot now. The cheery face of Beryl appeared before her, holding a sterilised pack containing a theatre gown. "Let me help you with this, pet. I'll open the outer paper of it without touching the inside, you then lift the gown out, only touching the inside of the gown that will go next to your body. Have you got that?" Sylvia nodded as she carefully slid her clean hands down the inside arms of the voluminous theatre gown. Beryl tied up the back fastenings, and then opened a pair of sterile latex gloves, revealing the inner sterile package. Sylvia put them on, tucking the ends of the sleeves into the gloves that snugly gripped her wrists. She realised she had forgotten to put on a face mask, but Beryl had already noticed, and approached her holding one. "Turn round, don't touch it. I'll put you this on and fasten it," she said.

Sylvia suddenly realised that Penny was nowhere to be seen, and was, as usual, late. She was ushered into the theatre space, feeling a bit like a spaceman walking into an alien landscape. She hadn't realised how many people were needed to support a

Caesarean section. Frankie Lyons, Senior Midwife, was assigned to theatre duty that day and she noticed the new student midwife trying not to be noticed. A large pair of blue eyes, filled with fear, peered out over the top of her face mask, and Frankie's heart melted with sympathy. She was fully scrubbed up, gown and mask on, standing by a trolley next to the theatre bed that was awash with instruments, her sterile hands encased in gloves. She caught Sylvia's eyes and gesticulated with her head for her to come closer. "Come and stand next to me," she said, at which the student, she noted, looked even more petrified than before, if that was possible.

Charles Ash, Anaesthetist, was not only very experienced at charming the legs off any female that caught his eye, and there were many, he was also very good at his job, a trait that had on a number of occasions saved his bacon with the Health Authority Board when misdemeanours with a variety of female staff had resulted in embarrassing situations reported by some individuals. Sister Frenchit came to mind as his nemesis. They had hated each other on sight and both, to onlookers anyway, seemed to take a diverse pleasure in rubbing each other the wrong way at every available opportunity. She had reported him for unprofessional conduct, when, after a ward round on her ward she had discovered him in the laundry supplies room at the end of the ward exploring in great detail a female member of staff's anatomy which, as she later complained to a retired colleague, could be seen in graphic detail in Margaret Myles's textbook on the anatomy and physiology of the female genital tract.

Today, however, his mind was most definitely centred on the patient lying on the trolley in front of him. She had been given a pre-med to help her relax before she was wheeled into the theatre and placed on the theatre bed. This was a planned Caesarean section, the decision made weeks ago when it was discovered that her afterbirth, or placenta, had decided to embed itself into the very lowest part of her uterus and not at the top or side, which was the usual. This was a diagnosis made by the consultant in charge of the case who had dealt with a number of cases where the presenting part of the baby, in this case the bottom as baby was a breech presentation, remained impossibly high in the pelvic cavity and did not fully descend down into the lower reaches of the pelvis. He had witnessed first-hand the catastrophic results of massive haemorrhage on the mother and baby, when, following dilation of the neck of the womb, the attached placenta had become unattached, resulting in the tearing of blood vessels that were attached to the lower part of the mother's uterus. With the baby and afterbirth still inside the uterus, contraction of the three muscle layers of the uterus that would normally have effectively sealed off the bleeding points could not happen, and as the blood supply to the uterus for obvious reasons was massive, the resulting haemorrhage was torrential and unmanageable with a baby still undelivered. Treatment was not to allow these women to go into labour, but to deliver them with a Caesarean section, which was the situation with the lady on the theatre bed.

Sylvia had learned that this condition of a low-lying placenta was called Placenta Praevia, which had varying degrees of severity. Some placentas were low lying but would allow a head or bottom to descend through the mother's bony pelvis. The worst sort, grade four, completely blocked any exit out of the pelvis.

Frankie Lyons stood on one side of the theatre bed, her sterile gloved hands clasped calmly in front of her, looking as if she was praying, but was in reality avoiding any contact at all with anything that could potentially de-sterilise her and result in her having to scrub from scratch all over again. She had asked Sylvia to stand opposite her, towards the lower end of the bed, so that they were facing each other across the mother's abdomen. She knew full well how nervous this student was and knew that the best way to get through the first time was to get her involved early on by helping in some small way and not just standing there observing. Frankie's job was to be the right-hand man of the obstetrician. She was in charge of an enormous tray of sterilised instruments, a variety of razor-sharp fine scalpels, a large pack of swabs that had had to be counted out and then the numbers chalked up on a board, suturing needles and a number of suturing cat guts and silks. Stainless-steel instruments were lined up in order of use onto the large trolley, along with a small bowl of bright pink liquid which had a bunch of swabs attached to long-handled forceps sitting in it.

Charles Ash prepared, after a nod from the consultant, to start the string of procedures that would result in his patient being completely anaesthetised. He plunged the end of the syringe in and ejected a fast-acting anaesthetic into the patient's blood stream via a venflon cannula that was situated for easy access into the vein in the back of her hand.

The patient was counting backwards from ten and had reached seven when her voice slurred and stopped. Quickly, he inserted a laryngoscope into her mouth, tipping her head back into a favourable position to do so, and then inserted a long thin tube down into her lungs that would be attached to an oxygen supply. His assistant attached the patient to a variety of monitors that would give crucial feedback on blood pressure, pulse, and the circulating amount of oxygen in the bloodstream, the patient's respiration rate, and more.

"Are we ready?" asked Richard Toft. He received a curt nod from Charles Ash, and then he picked up a scalpel offered to him by Frankie.

Sylvia's palms inside her sterile rubber gloves were wet with sweat, as was her brow. She hadn't realised how hot it would be under the mountain of theatre lights, not to mention being encased in a uniform, plastic apron on top of her starched apron, and then a green sterile gown over the top of the lot. She watched fearfully as Frankie took hold of the forceps that held swabs in the pink liquid and proceeded to wipe from the patient's lower rib cage across and down to the Symphysis pubis which had been shaved clean of any pubic hair. Richard Toft could not perform the usual lower transverse incision in the skin, from side to side, just above the Symphysis pubis because if he had, he would have sliced through not only abdominal muscles and the wall of the uterus, but straight through the placenta as well and so he needed to use a classical incision that was much higher up and longitudinal, not transverse.

Sylvia braced herself as Richard pushed the scalpel's point gently, oh so gently, into the skin, and pulled down in a straight line. Immediately a thin pink line appeared, as if drawn on by a red biro, and blood began to trickle. Frankie swabbed as Richard opened up his incision even more, exposing the Rectus Abdominis muscles beneath the skin. Sylvia became aware of Frankie's eyes looking at her.

"When I tell you, make sure you put all the used swabs in that bowl at your feet. Make sure you touch nothing at all except the swabs." Sylvia nodded, scared and mesmerised at the same time as the peritoneum, a thin white skin covering the outside of the uterus, became visible to her eyes. She knew what it was as they had been taught the anatomy of the uterus in their first few weeks in the large classroom. Rivulets of blood were being sucked away by Frankie who was using an electrical sucker, and stored in a container that measured the amount of blood loss. Richard used his fingers to gently separate even further the two halves of one of the abdominal muscles and exposed the pregnant uterus. Sylvia was amazed at the compactness of it, how smooth, how vascular. It was like looking at a large, pink balloon. She could see for the first time deep inside someone's body, the workings of it all, and she forgot her fears. How could a baby fit inside there alongside a placenta as big as a dinner plate and all that fluid, which she had learned was called liquor amnii?

She became aware of someone standing close and realised it was the Paediatrician getting in position, ready to take the baby over to the rescusitaire unit as soon as it was delivered. Amazement was replacing the fear as she watched Richard incise into the uterus. There was a spurt of a yellow liquid as he inserted a hand into the incision and then slowly pulled out a tiny pink arm, waving, with fingers splayed wide which then magically, for a second, found Richard's thumb and closed tightly around it. Seconds later a head, then another arm and shoulders, and then he was lifting the baby up and out, onto a towel that was being held out by a theatre auxiliary nurse. "Ergometrine, please," he instructed, as an intramuscular injection to help the uterus contract was given into the mother's thigh. The baby's airways were being sucked out by an assistant at the side of the theatre bed and his cord clamped and cut by Frankie at the same time. The whole episode was over so quickly that Sylvia felt she had dreamt all of it. She also understood that she had witnessed a procedure honed countless times by a whole team who knew exactly what each other's roles were. They knew their own boundaries of care, their own professional responsibilities and limitations, all adhering to their own codes of practice with just one aim in mind: the safe delivery of a mother and baby.

Suddenly Richard paused. "Placenta Acretia," he said, and the theatre became silent. They all knew what that meant - the next few minutes and their actions would be crucial. Most placentas separate as the uterus contracts after delivery of the baby, but with Placenta Acretia they are, sometimes, morbidly attached and so deeply embedded into the sidewall of the uterus that they literally have to be scraped off. In the meantime, the recipient begins to bleed massively as the uterus is unable to contract effectively to seal off any bleeding points as the placenta is still attached. In some cases, a hysterectomy has to be performed to save a mother's life. Sylvia was unaware of the obstetric emergency about to unfold in front of her eyes. She noticed the sudden stillness and drop in professional banter between staff as Richard, who appeared to be struggling in achieving delivery of the placenta, calmly said,

"Get more units cross matched, now, site an IV in

the other arm, we need a unit going through in each arm, and get more swab." Sweat was beginning to form on his brow as he delicately continued to inch by inch peel the placenta away.

"Blood pressure's dropping." This from Charles Ash who had rapidly inserted another drip line and was, by hand Sylvia noted with astonishment, holding and beginning to actually squeeze the blood bag to speed up the flow of blood through the tubing and into the patient. Sylvia looked down and realised that blood was beginning to seep over the edge of the theatre bed, even though Frankie was using the mechanical suction machine. "Blood pressure still dropping, pulse rising, pushing blood volume expander, IV being given now," said Charles Ash, who was rapidly drawing up a series of substances into syringes as well as inserting yet another venous infusion into the patient's arm. Sister Francis was using up packet after packet of large sterile gauze swabs which were soaked immediately, and Sylvia, aware of the importance of collecting them, began to gather them after use and drop them into a stainless-steel bowl that was on the floor by her feet. Richard continued to try to peel the placenta of the uterine wall and let out an expletive that Sister Frenchit would most definitely not approve of. He had managed with great difficulty to separate most of the placenta, and as he peeled back the last section, it began to tear. If any tissue was left inside the uterus it could cause infection and also the uterus would not be able to contact properly and control any bleeding. He had pulled out the vast majority of an organ that was a life-giving miracle of function and form, giving the gift of life to a baby, and yet it equally could be responsible for the death of a mother.

"Not on my shift, not on my fucking shift," he muttered to himself. With renewed vigour he concentrated on the section that was refusing to give, and breathed a huge sigh of relief as the last bit of placental tissue came away in his hands. Sylvia's gloved hands were covered in blood as she concentrated on collecting the bloodied swabs into the bowl at her feet. If the swab count at the end did not tally with how many swabs had been opened and used, there was a risk that one or more may have been left inside a body, and Sylvia could see from what she had just witnessed how very easily that could happen.

Richard finally had begun to suture the layers of the uterine muscle back together again with symmetry and co-ordination born of long practice and, as Sylvia observed him, the anatomy and physiology lectures that she had attended so far began to consolidate and make a lot more sense. Actually, being able to see a uterus inside the pelvic cavity, to see the muscle layers and where they were attached to the sidewalls of the pelvic cavity made it much easier to connect to the anatomy lectures that they frequently attended.

The atmosphere had lightened considerably in the theatre once the placenta had been delivered. The blood flow from the patient had slowed considerably and both obstetrician and anaesthetist were happier with their patient's clinical observations. Thirty minutes later, the last of the abdominal skin sutures were in place. Richard stepped back as the theatre staff continued to monitor the patient's vital signs. When they were happy, they would prepare to transfer the patient back to a room on the labour ward where she would stay for at least another twenty-four hours. She had lost a lot of blood and would need careful monitoring. He peeled down his mask, took off his gloves, and threw them into a clinical waste basket. He flexed his shoulder muscles and winked at Frankie.

"We don't want too many of those, do we, Sister Lyons?"

"No, Mr Toft, we certainly don't," responded Frankie, who by this time was showing Sylvia where all the used swabs had been hung as they had been collected throughout the time the Caesarean section had been underway.

"I don't know about you, but I reckon we've earned a drink. Go get yourself one while I write the notes up and I'll see you then," said Frankie.

Sylvia went back to the changing-room and sat quietly for a few minutes, thinking about what she had just witnessed. She had seen the beginning of another new life, the potential ending of another's life if not for the skill of those staff in the theatre, routine surgery performed many times that turned into an unexpected nightmare for a few hours, with a potential ending that she couldn't bear thinking about. She had remained incredibly calm in the theatre, watching the scene unfold, working on auto-pilot as Frankie told her what to do, how to do it, when to do it. The fear of seeing incisions into the abdomen had been subsumed by the amazing spectacle of the anatomy of the human body, and the collective exhilaration of all the staff when the patient's condition stabilised. She had been standing in theatre for three hours and realised why she was feeling so shaky. She changed back into her uniform, walked out of theatre, down the corridor, and embraced the delights of tea and toast.

Chapter Five

Sylvia was in the staff sitting-room on the labour ward, going through a set of notes with Sister Francis. She was trying to get to grips with the anatomy of the pelvic floor and was finding it difficult. She had seen Sister Francis performing an episiotomy on the lady whose delivery she had just witnessed, and could not comprehend the fact that at some point in her career, if she ever got that far, she would also be asked to take a pair of scissors and cut through layers of skin and muscle, albeit that you were also skilled enough to numb the area adequately first with a large syringe of local anaesthetic. She had been practising various techniques that helped students of anatomy remember the avalanche of information about the body and pregnancy that was pushed at them daily, not only in the classroom, but at the patient's bedside too. The most senior midwifery tutor, Mrs O'Neil, who was Irish, four-feet-ten inches tall, blessed with an acerbic wit and piercing grey eyes that missed nothing, had spent the previous afternoon teaching them the detailed anatomy and physiology of the pelvic floor, a subject that would need to be known as well as their own face if they were to practise Midwifery. She taught daily in what was called The Large Classroom, sited over the antenatal clinic on the first floor and her lectures were legendary. Mrs O'Neil would also meet them on the wards and would choose a patient to examine and discuss with each student, talking them through the notes and showing them how to palpate a pregnant abdomen, diagnose a variety of abnormalities, and discuss modes and methods of treatment. Penny Jones had already been the unwilling participant in one of Mrs O'Neil's methods of dealing with students who dared to talk, or whisper, during her lectures. On one memorable occasion Penny had been admonished for talking yet again and then been told to stand at the front of the classroom. The whole student group looked on in astonishment as Mrs O'Neil took a large white sheet, asked Penny to hold out both arms at her side, shoulder level, and then proceeded to drape the sheet over the top of her head, arms, and body, with the sheet touching the ground. The whole room was silent as they gazed upon a white ghostly form of Penny standing before them.

"Today," said Mrs O'Neil in a matter-of-fact voice, "we are going to learn about the broad ligament, a large white sheaf of connective tissue that inhabits the pelvic regions, and we will learn about the connective tissue that separately covers each of our internal organs. Miss Jones here is that broad ligament." Stifled sniggers could be heard from various parts of the classroom, which were instantly silenced by a piercing look from Mrs O'Neil. The lecture continued for another ten minutes, students silently listening, all desperate to laugh, but no one daring. From that day on, Penny and everyone else did not chat in Mrs O'Neil's lectures and other bemused Midwifery tutors puzzled frequently as to why this particular group of student Midwives all got top marks in their latest written assignment on the pelvic anatomy and physiology and especially that of the broad ligament!

Sister Francis was signing off Sylvia's observations record book when the labour ward suite coordinator came into the sitting-room.

"Is your lady ready for warding now?" she asked Sister Francis, to which Sister Francis nodded as she swallowed the last of her tea.

"A phone call's come in from one of the housing

estates. There's a young girl, getting ready to push, and there's no community midwife near. Can you get out to her, with a delivery pack. The ambulance is on its way to pick you up now."

Sister Francis stood, grabbed her woollen cloak, and said, "Right, Nurse Ayres, fancy a ride in the back of an ambulance? Come on, get a move on, we need to pick up bags and packs from the Central Sterilising stock cupboard. We need portable Entonox too if she's well on in labour."

Four minutes later, with a pile of bags at their feet, they were standing under the canopy of the main entrance to the maternity unit, and Sylvia saw an ambulance speed round the corner and stop in front them. The driver helped them and their equipment into the back of the ambulance and closed the rear doors on them as they seated themselves inside, on each side on the built-in patient trolleys. The ambulance accelerated, and the driver turned on the blue flashing lights; they were on their way. The seats in the back were hard and the ambulance's suspension left a lot to be desired. Sylvia was swung from side to side and had to really concentrate on staying upright as the driver took corners on what she swore later were just two wheels. The noise of the siren was deafening, and she was sure she had seen via the back window that they had gone through a number of red lights.

The address was a well-known council estate, about five miles away that Sylvia had heard a lot about from the other Midwives. For some strange reason, the local council had chosen to house every problem family in the city all together in a couple of notorious trouble spots across the city, and this estate was one of them. She felt really excited about this unexpected experience in the community; this was real midwifery in the home setting, baby deciding to arrive a bit faster for all concerned, but in the bosom of a loving family.

"This will be a useful experience for you, showing you how we adapt our practice to a community setting, where you don't have all mod cons to hand. I may need to send you to find a telephone if we encounter any problems," said Sister Francis. "It's very unlikely this address will have a telephone."

Sylvia concentrated on hanging onto a support strap on the bed in the ambulance as the ambulance went around some more corners on two wheels. She was flung sideways at each turn and thought at some point that she might end up on the floor and be the one who needed clinical intervention, and not the young girl they were on their way to see. Sister

Francis seemed to have an uncanny sense of balance, as she sat calmly checking the contents of her bags, checking drugs that might be needed were still in date for use. At last the ambulance braked, came to a stop, and the back doors were flung open. Grabbing a nursing bag, a sort of hold-all packed with a variety of sterile dressings, spare instrument packs and other yet-to-be recognised tools of the trade, Sylvia stepped down into the street, helping Sister Francis with the other equipment. The house they were to visit was easily recognised as all the lights were on, and a small group of neighbours had gathered around the front gate. A path led up to the front door, winding its way through a garden that looked more like a rubbish tip. There were piles of rubbish rubbing shoulders with a couple of pairs of old rusty bikes, old bits of carpet, and two bins overflowing against a wall. There was a lad, who looked to be no more than fifteen years old, who was standing, smoking, by the front door, slouched against the doorway, grubby jeans and teeshirt wrinkled, bare footed.

"Yer too late, she's add it," he informed Sister Francis, who never broke her stride.

"Where is she?"

"Up there." He pointed up the stairs, and Sister

Francis took the steps two at a time with Sylvia valiantly trying to keep up. At the top of the stairs was a woman who Sylvia supposed was the boy's mother.

"She's in here, duck, on the bed."

She led the way into a dingy bedroom where there was no wallpaper on the walls, a filthy carpet covered the floor and the smell almost made Sylvia heave. On the bed lay a girl who looked about the same age as the boy downstairs. She wore a blood-stained short nightgown and lay on a pile of grubby-looking sheets that had rucked up to show a wad of sanitary pads tucked in between her legs. She was strangely quiet. Sister Francis quickly examined the pads, estimating blood loss as she did so and laid a hand on the mother's abdomen, checking that the uterus was contracted, as she asked, "Where's the baby?" in a tone that Sylvia had not heard before.

"It's in here," said the woman who had greeted them at the bottom of the stairs, and she led them across the landing to a bathroom that was equally derelict. The bath was filthy and looked as if no one had ever bathed in it. Sylvia was shocked by what she was seeing. She was appalled at the state of the house which was filthy in a way she had never experienced before. Torn wallpaper on the walls, a single dim light bulb with no shade, and there was no sign of any baby things anywhere, there was no sign even of a cot. Everyone was very silent. The boy at the doorway had stayed downstairs, lighting up a cigarette, showing no interest in the events taking place a few yards away. The woman pointed to the toilet.

"I told her to get off, but she wouldn't, she kept on pushing, there was nowt I could do," the woman said in a belligerent tone. Sylvia had never seen Sister Francis move so fast as she grabbed a pair of gloves, pushed aside the woman, and almost ran across the landing. As she approached the toilet, she kneeled down in front of it.

"Go and stay with your daughter, will you?" Sister Francis said to the woman. To Sylvia she said,

"Nurse Ayres, go and open the delivery pack and bring me the towel that's inside. Be quick, and bring my nursing bag too."

Sylvia returned in seconds to witness a scene that would stay with her for the rest of her life. Sister Francis was kneeling, with her arm down the toilet, and slowly, as she lifted her arm, it became obvious that she was holding something, a small, perfect little baby by the ankles, covered in blood, with his cord and placenta still attached. It was a boy baby who Sister Francis knew by experience weighed about four pounds. Sylvia could not tear her eyes away from the still form. Despair, horror, sadness all fought to take control as she visibly paled and stood rooted to the spot.

"Pass me the towel, Nurse Ayres," said Sister Francis quietly, breaking the silence which lay like a cloak over everything. Sylvia laid the towel on the floor by the toilet and Sister Francis put on it a little boy whose only taste of life had been the months inside his mother's womb. She swaddled him in the towel so tenderly that Sylvia became choked with emotion and shook with the effort of trying not to sob. Standing, she placed the baby into Sylvia's arms so tenderly, like a precious piece of porcelain that could disintegrate at any given moment.

"Stay with him whilst I go and talk to the mother and grandmother," and then, "are you OK with that?"

Sylvia nodded, unable to talk, and once Sister Francis had left the bathroom, she cried, her chest heaving in the effort to try and remain unheard in her grief. Her cheeks became sore with the saltiness of her tears. The little still form looked so alone that she could bear it no longer. She carefully nursed him in her arms, the ache in her chest wrapping like a tight band around her torso.

"I thought Midwifery was about life, little one," she whispered, as tears dripped onto his towel. "I've learned a new lesson today."

She could hear Sister Francis talking to the mother, grandmother, and the father of the baby who, it turned out, was the boy standing on the step. She could hear no sounds of distress or tears from them, and she started as suddenly the bathroom door opened and Sister Francis entered.

"I need to go and find a phone box, and ring the police," she explained. "I cannot remove a dead body from a house without a coroner's or police permission, in case of foul play." She went on to reassure Sylvia that mum's condition was satisfactory, all her observations normal, and at a later time they would be transferring both mum and the baby back to the labour ward in the ambulance. Sylvia pulled the toilet seat down and sat on it, still holding the baby.

"She doesn't want to see the baby, none of them do," explained Sister Francis. "So will you be OK for a few more minutes?" Sylvia looked down at the tiny bundle in her arms and looked at Sister Francis.

"How could they not want to see him?" she whispered. "How could they?"

"We will talk about this later," said Sister Francis

briskly. "I need to sort a few things out. Are you OK here, with baby for a little while?"

Sylvia nodded and clutched the tiny still form a little closer to her chest. As the bathroom door closed behind her, her tears dripped of the end of her nose and onto the baby so tenderly held against her chest. She sat in the bathroom nursing and rocking, quietly talking into a little shell-like ear that would never hear her words of endearment.

Twenty minutes later, Sister Francis was back and, shortly after, no less than six policemen and two officers from CID arrived and filled the house with their presence. They interviewed everyone in the house and examined the baby so often that Sylvia began to feel angry on his behalf, wanting them to just leave him in peace.

Finally, hours later, they were finished, and the mother and baby were put into the back of the ambulance, with Sister Francis, Sylvia, and equipment in tow. The young mother, it turned out, had concealed her pregnancy and so missed most of her antenatal care, and then defaulted most of her other clinic appointments as well. Sylvia's emotional frame of mind was in turmoil as she vacillated between anger at the perceived indifference from the family about what had happened, and compassion and sorrow for a young mother whose chances in life and support from her family seemed very limited.

It was a slow, sombre ride back to the hospital. Sylvia sat on one side, opposite the mother, still holding the tiny form in her arms. It had seemed disrespectful to do anything, except what she was now doing which was giving this baby what should have been his birthright: close, physical, loving contact with another person. She had watched as Sister Francis had talked quietly to the young mother, again asking if she wanted to see or hold her baby, but she had adamantly refused, shaking her head and turning away from them both. The ambulance was greeted at the hospital entrance with porters who helped to transfer the mother onto a trolley and then she was pushed through the hospital's main entrance, and down the corridor to a labour room. The baby was handed over to another member of staff who then arranged for transfer to the hospital morgue where a post-mortem would be carried out as soon as possible.

Sylvia felt drained. Two hours later she sat in the sitting-room on the labour ward, clutching a mug of tea, facing Sister Francis, who was desperately trying to catch up on the obligatory note keeping. There was so much that she had to record, and she knew how important it was that her notes were accurate and written as soon as possible. She had talked to Sylvia, witnessed further tears, reassured her that her tears were not a sign of weakness and not coping, and spelt out the lessons that she had learned that day.

"Dealing with the death of a mother or a baby underlines the importance of the work we do," she explained gently. "It would be impossible to practise Midwifery without, at some point having to deal with it. This is what we are trying to avoid when we carry out all of our routine observations, when we monitor pregnancies, why we have antenatal wards full of high-risk pregnancies. You think it should be all about life, and mostly it is, but we also have to deal with it when the outcome is not a happy one. These will be your skills, you will learn to be strong for the parents, and their babies, whatever their circumstances, and then you will go off duty, and either celebrate or grieve with them in your own way, at home."

Years later, Sylvia reflected on the experiences of that day and what it had taught her. She learned to appreciate even more, if that was possible, the beauty and the precious gift of life and she quietly, mentally, said a little prayer of thanks for the gift of life at the birth of every baby she had the pleasure of delivering from that day on.

Chapter Six

Ever since Penny had witnessed Debbie Mathews in a state of undress with that consultant anaesthetist in the basement changing-rooms, she had done her utmost to keep out of her way. Why she should feel so embarrassed about the whole thing she had no idea. After all, it wasn't her who had cavorted in such an unseemly manner. Debbie Mathews was working on the labour ward suite and was frequently in charge. She was a very experienced Midwife, though Penny in unguarded moments raised her eyes sarcastically and hinted there was more than Midwifery that she was experienced in! She did, however, hold a grudging respect for her knowledge and skills, which were impeccable.

Penny was slowly acclimatising to her role as a student midwife, but she hadn't found it easy, not like her friend Sylvia who had taken to it all like a duck to water. She smiled as she thought about Sylvia and hoped fervently that she could keep up with everything that was being asked of her. She was painfully aware that she needed to work harder than some of her group, and she was determined to get through her training, come what may. She had a good friend in Sylvia, the best. She would patiently sit and explain to her any part of the anatomy lectures that she was struggling to understand, and they would sit for hours over a cup of coffee, with a copy of Margaret Myles' textbook on Midwifery in front of them, testing each other. It was a great tomb of a book, lavishly illustrated, and at the moment the only book on their horizon for the next two years. She, Sylvia, and Rosie Smith had quickly established a rapport that was to last them throughout the whole of their careers, little did they know it yet.

Penny had been assigned to work in a small ward area called Progress, right next to and adjoining the labour ward suite. It was here that women in labour were admitted to be assessed, where general practitioners who had concerns about their pregnant patients sent them in for a medical review and where community Midwives could also directly admit their community patients if they had any concerns about them. Women who came in from home in spontaneous labour were admitted and spent a large part of their labour in the Progress department. When they were well on in labour, sometimes wanting to push, they were transferred around the corner to the labour ward suite to deliver their babies. Midwives were often seen doing a mad dash down the corridor, pushing a trolley, husband in tow, trying not to have a woman deliver in the corridor! Sometimes it was a close call, especially if there were no empty labour rooms and women had had to wait longer in Progress than anticipated.

Women who were to have an induction of labour came from the wards to Progress, where an intravenous infusion with a drug called syntocinon was slowly administered over a few hours, helping to prepare the neck of the womb for labour and inducing contractions.

Penny was delighted to learn that her friend Sylvia was also rostered to work on Progress that morning where a large number of induction cases were coming down from the wards to be started off in labour. Her job was to prep these ladies prior to them having a drip sited in their arm. This 'prep' consisted of giving each lady a full pubic shave followed by an enema, and then a nice warm bath. The shave was to ensure as clean an area as possible for the delivery and also for the obstetric staff to have a clear view of all the tissues around the entrance to the woman's body. An enema was also given to empty the bowel of any faeces, helping to preserve the cleanliness of the delivery area and it was thought to help stimulate contractions. It was known that the nerve plexus supply to the whole perineal area and uterus was connected. Stimulation of one area also impacted upon the other areas too, and the giving of an enema helped to stimulate weaker irregular contractions onto greater heights. Penny had performed a number of shaves and was feeling confident.

She put on a plastic apron to protect her uniform and set up her shave trolley. She manoeuvred it with great difficulty between the bed and the wall area. She pulled across the curtains that surrounded the bed on which lay the lady she had to prepare for induction. The lady in question was no stranger to the maternity unit as she had had four previous children but was now overdue by about ten days. Penny explained to the mother what she was about to do. She then pulled the covers back, tucked an incontinence sheet under the woman's torso, and asked her to put her feet together flat on the bed and to please open her knees wide, ready for the shave to commence. Penny's patient had once been an avid motorcycle fan and boasted a large amount of not very well-executed tattoos on various parts of her body. There were at least three hearts with arrows with different male names attached to them, streaming banners with names of motorcycle brands and a few skulls thrown in for good measure. Around her neck was tattooed a chain with a padlock attached, which read, 'Take me, I'm yours'.

Penny put on a pair of rubber gloves and picked up the can of shaving foam from the trolley. She was feeling really confident with this procedure as she had successfully carried out a number of them recently. The issues surrounding her own code of modesty, dignity, and the nuances of the naked human body were still a difficulty to be surmounted but she was getting there. Aiming the can's nozzle, she pressed firmly down to release some foam, and nothing happened. She pressed again but still nothing. Cursing quietly behind her mask she gave the can a good shake and jabbed the top of the can once more. An exploding snowfall of shaving foam shot out with the force of Mount Vesuvius and to Penny's horror covered not only the woman's pubic area, but the bed, her nightdress, and the woman's face. It was everywhere and, to make matters worse, the button on top of the can had jammed and was still spewing out foam like a tidal wave.

"Oh God, no!" shouted Penny and she aimed the

still-spraying can down towards the mattress. Sylvia, who was next door prepping her lady, heard the commotion and stuck her head around the curtain to see what was going on. The sight that met her eyes was the talk of the coffee room for the next month as Penny tried in vain to stop the can from spraying. It was unfortunate that Mrs O'Neil, senior Midwifery tutor, chose that exact moment to check on how the new students in Progress area were doing. She pulled the curtain back and startled Penny so much that she dropped the can which rolled under the bed and continued to spray out, finally spluttering to a stop.

The bed area looked like someone had sprayed a foam fire extinguisher on it. The ensuing silence could have been cut with a knife.

Mrs O'Neil raised her eyes heavenward and exclaimed, 'Jesus, Mary, Mother of God. Well, Nurse Jones, you have excelled yourself this time." Sylvia, who was still standing open-mouthed by the curtain, couldn't help but notice that there was a definite twinkle in her eyes as she said it.

Mrs O'Neil called for Mercy, the cleaning lady for the ward area, to come and help clean the foam away whilst Penny apologised profusely to her patient who had stayed remarkably calm throughout the whole episode. Still apologising, Penny found a facecloth and wiped the excess foam away from her patient's face and glasses and changed her bed sheets and hospital gown. Finally, Penny was ready to start again. Mrs O'Neil was seen a few minutes later walking back down the corridor, shaking her head, her shoulders shaking with mirth, wiping some moisture from her eyes.

Penny's memories of that encounter were not quite over as with a new, tested can of spray foam, she got on with the job of shaving the lady's pubic area. As the hairy growth was slowly removed in a slather of foam, the form of another tattoo was slowly revealed. It was an arrow, pointing downwards, sitting on top of the fleshy mound of her symphysis pubis, along with the words 'this way in.'

Chapter Seven

The Maternity unit was situated in the grounds of what had originally been a Victorian workhouse and the old City General Hospital, built in various phases of development throughout the last one hundred years or so, now surrounding the very recently built Maternity Unit. It stuck out like a sore thumb with its modern steel and glass six floors, a typical design of the many buildings being built in the nineteen-sixties.

A huge canopy covered the main entrance so that ambulances could discharge their patients protected from the elements. There were two lifts on the ground floor, through the main reception, that were used by patients and staff alike, and this had resulted in some interesting scenarios over the years when visitors and patients had competed for space or priority in the lifts. This happened when obstetric emergencies were being transferred from one of the six floors downstairs to the labour ward or theatres, which were based on the ground floor. The visitors getting in on floor six may have their descent down in the lift interrupted on floor two by Midwives pushing a trolley into the confined space with a lady whose induction and early labour had accelerated rather more rapidly than anticipated and who was now wanting to push! It was not unknown for the odd delivery to take place in the lift.

It was on floor six that the General Practitioner Unit was based. Commonly known as the GPU, women who had very low-risk pregnancies and labours were booked for delivery by Midwives or sometime by General Practitioners who wanted to deliver their own patients. Labouring women would be admitted, cared for, delivered, and then given post-natal care for ten to twelve days or more if needed. The most senior person present at the deliveries was the Midwife. If any abnormality or high-risk pregnancy or labour was detected, then medical aid or advice would be sought and the patient would be transferred to the care of a consultant and moved to a different ward. It was on this ward that Sylvia and Penny were presently working. All deliveries were low risk and normal, women coming in from home in spontaneous labour. There were no beeping monitors, drip stands, or monitoring machines, no demanding Consultants or senior registrars, no lab technicians bringing in equipment or taking samples, just an all-pervading calm and peacefulness, broken occasionally by a buzzer request or a baby's cry. That is not to say that it didn't get busy up there because when it was busy it was really busy. Often two or three labouring women with just one Midwife and an auxiliary nurse to assist was not unusual.

No one can predict when a woman will go into labour so manpower planning in terms of staff numbers on duty at any one time was always notoriously difficult. Auxiliary nurses and nursery nurses provided invaluable and skilful support and close teamwork was needed as much on this unit as it was needed in the busy labour rooms and theatres on the ground floor, far below.

Sylvia was standing by the desk, stationed in the centre of the ward area, looking at the daybook. The daybook was the contemporaneous working document of the day that was continuously updated with results, comments, and instructions. It was also a ward diary with a list of patients who were inpatients on the ward that day. It showed exactly where each patient was, giving her name, room number, and bed number. It would also show what type of delivery, how many days delivered she was, and if she was bottle or breast-feeding. Sylvia and Penny had just finished doing the bed-making round. Twenty-two beds all needing a top and tail, and that were just if the bottom sheet and frequently soiled smaller incontinence sheet needed changing. Women who had gone home had their beds completely stripped and the whole bed, frame and mattress included, would be washed down in an antiseptic solution. Like the scrub procedure for putting on sterile gloves, there was a routine method of how the bed was washed and how it was made up too. The bed round, as it was commonly known, was one of the first duties allocated to the students after listening to the ward report from night staff who would be handing the shift over to the day staff coming on duty in the morning. The students were really slick and quick at bedmaking now, much to the amazement of their mothers who both professed that bedmaking was a first in their daughter's lives!

There were other rounds too that soon became as easy and practised as breathing in and out, such as blood pressure rounds or TPR rounds where every woman's temperature, pulse, and respirations were noted and documented daily.

The telephone on the nurse station desk rang, and Barbara the ward clerk answered it. She was a cheery soul who had worked on the ward for years and could always be relied upon to work unsupervised and get the job done. She listened intently, scribbled some information down on a notepad, and walked briskly down the corridor to find the Midwife in charge saying, as she did so to the two students:

"There's a lady on the way up in the lift, well on in labour. If you need to witness more deliveries this one is imminent. I'll tell the Midwife if you want to witness this one." Each student in their first year of training had to witness a minimum of forty deliveries and so it became quite competitive if there were lots of students in a ward area at any one time that all wanted to witness the same procedure. Usually only one or a maximum of two were allowed with the permission of the parents. Both students were delighted that another delivery could be ticked off in their delivery witness books. They walked briskly down to the end of the ward where the labour room was sited and opened a delivery pack, sterile glove pack, and sterile green gown, ready for the Midwife who would be conducting the case. The heater over the baby rescusitaire was switched on and oxygen supplies checked.

Both students hurried back up the corridor to Sister's office where sets of notes for women who were known to be due soon were filed. Each woman had her own unique reference number on her notes and the students soon found the set for the lady who was on her way up to them. They returned to the desk area where Sister Hobson, who was in charge of the GPU, had just put the phone back down again. They all turned in unison to the sound of the lift door opening, and the sounds coming out of it.

A rather beautiful lady, dressed in a colourful sari and noticeably heavily pregnant, was being wheeled out of the lift in a wheelchair towards the glass double doors leading to the ward area.

The amount of moaning and wailing coming from her was at such a pitch that it drowned out any of the words that the poor unfortunate father was trying to speak as he valiantly manoeuvred the wheelchair from the lift through the doors. It became immediately obvious that the couple spoke very little, if any, English and also that this lady was about to give birth at any moment. She was making sounds in her throat that Sister Hobson knew from the experience of hundreds of previous deliveries boded the arrival of a baby in minutes, not hours.

Sister Hobson took charge, gesticulating to the father to push his wife quickly down the corridor to the labour ward, saying to the students as they almost ran in their haste,

"Get a gown and a mask for the dad and one of you start opening the delivery pack, quickly now we haven't got much time." They reached the labour room door almost at a run as the lady started to push; deep guttural sounds, long and drawn out, erupting from her throat. Her head was thrown back and the veins stood out in her neck as her body took control of the birthing process, involuntary pushing becoming continuous. The father was at this point gesticulating wildly as Penny attempted, with great difficulty, to wrap the obligatory voluminous green gown around him and to put a face mask onto his face. The wheelchair had been pushed through the door with the labouring mother barely on the seat. She was by now so intent on pushing and bearing down that she had ceased listening to any instructions given, regardless of the fact that she also spoke no English and was lying half off the wheelchair. With a combined superhuman effort they managed to get her onto the delivery bed. The wheelchair had effectively trapped Mr Patel up the corner by the bed head, and Mrs Patel was gripping his hand so tightly it reminded Sylvia of her first birth experience all those months ago. Mrs Patel was wearing a gorgeous silk sari with matching pantaloons. They were removed in record time by Sister Hobson who realised she would be lucky to get a pair of gloves on in time, let alone set out a nice sterile delivery pack. Sylvia reached for a warm towel and Penny positioned the delivery pack on the end of the bed, as with one mighty push and a stream of unintelligible Punjabi from both parents, the baby's head crowned and was delivered, followed rapidly by the delivery of a lovely, plump little body. The baby cried immediately, the mother followed suit and both students breathed a sigh of relief. Baby's cord was cut and clamped and was then wrapped up warmly in a towel. As Penny handed him over to his mother, she was surprised to see dad standing back and showing no interest whatsoever in his baby. He looked a bit traumatised and kept running his hand through his hair and repeating something that she didn't understand. He did not attempt to approach his wife or baby. Considering the chaotic circumstances of the birth, Sylvia was not surprised he seemed a bit overwhelmed.

Barbara, efficient as ever, had seen in the notes that Mr and Mrs Patel spoke little English and had managed to get hold of an interpreter who was based on the antenatal clinic downstairs. She popped her head through the door to let Sister Hobson, who was just finishing delivering the afterbirth, know that she had arrived.

"Barbara, can you take this wheelchair out now so Mr Patel can get a good look at his lovely son? And before you do, can you ask the interpreter to explain to him that I need to put in just a couple of small stitches and could he tell his wife. It shouldn't take long."

The interpreter stepped smartly into the room. She was quite new in the job but was thoroughly enjoying working in the maternity unit. She approached Mr Patel and a rapid dialogue took place between them. It was Sylvia who first noticed that something was not quite right. The interpreter drew in a sharp breath, paled visibly, her eyes wide with shock. Mr Patel was by now gesticulating with both arms and pointing at Mrs Patel and the baby. His wife was the picture of contentment, nursing her baby and making little cooing sounds at him.

"Is there a problem?" asked Sister Hobson, looking up over her wire-rimmed glasses.

The interpreter gulped and said, "I don't quite know how to tell you this, Sister."

The interpreter now had the full attention of both students and Sister Hobson.

"He's not the father, he's just the taxi-driver who

brought her in."

There was a stunned silence in the room, broken only by the sounds of Mrs Patel cooing delightfully at her baby.

Everyone in the room turned to look at the hapless taxi-driver who had unwittingly been dragged in to witness a complete stranger's birth and who was now struggling to remove his gown and mask.

"He says he tried to tell you, but no one understood and then he couldn't get out of the room because of the wheelchair and then it was too late."

The interpreter spent the next twenty minutes apologising profusely to the taxi-driver who couldn't get away fast enough. Sister Hobson mused for some time on how to explain in the delivery notes that an unknown taxi-driver was present in the delivery room of a woman who was not his wife.

And both students, later, in the privacy of the linen cupboard laughed until their sides ached. The incident was from that day onwards locked forever in the annals of the maternity unit's history.

Chapter Eight

Sylvia was working on the antenatal clinic and slowly coming to understand the different consultants' protocols for caring for their patients. There were myriads of tests to learn about and practical sessions in what was known as The Blood Room where pregnant women would be sent for blood tests. This was where skills were honed through eight-hour shifts of doing nothing but just taking bloods and learning what coloured sample bottle to put them in. At first, she really struggled. Finding someone's vein in order to take a blood sample looked so easy as she watched experienced state-enrolled nurses never fail to find the right place. She finally realised that patience and a sensitive touch was the key to finding the exact spot to put the needle in. Gently feeling with a fingertip would almost always reveal a slight change in contour on the skin, ever so slightly raised where a bulging blood vessel was begging to be punctured, and eventually she developed an uncanny ability to find the right spot for the needle.

Many of the women who attended the antenatal clinic were high-risk pregnancies. Some women had medical problems as well as being pregnant. The medical consultant alongside the consultant obstetrician would manage cases of women with heart disease, diabetes, or kidney dysfunction.

The examination couches at the back of the clinic were where Midwives prepared women before the consultant saw them. Their blood pressure would be taken, urine sample tested, and then each woman would be weighed. Sylvia enjoyed working with women who were to be seen at the clinic and examined on the examination couches. She learned so much in that department as hundreds of women came through the doors each day, all with their own unique pregnancy problems and it wasn't just Midwifery problems that had to be sorted. Sylvia soon discovered that what was going on in a woman's personal or social life often impacted on her pregnancy too. Only last week she had seen a woman who was a heroin addict, and another woman whose husband was violent. The Midwives were continually accessing other areas of support for their patients and ringing social workers or the drug rehabilitation team, the council housing department, or the department for Sexually Transmitted Diseases.

Midwifery tutors could often be seen cruising along the row of examination cubicles, taking a student aside to discuss women's case notes or discussing and questioning the treatment for this and that.

One of the most important skills for all Midwives was the ability to be able to palpate a pregnant uterus. It involved following a precise procedure when laying hands onto a pregnant woman's abdomen and allowed the Midwife to discern lots of crucial, important information. There was only one way in which to become skilled and accurate when performing this type of examination and that was to literally perform hundreds and hundreds of such examinations with experienced Midwives. Student Midwives had to carry out at least fifty and document every one, having first been assessed with the accuracy of them by a qualified Midwife. Many important decisions were made following an abdominal palpation and it was absolutely crucial that the information was correct as it had impacts on the decisions made and the outcome of a pregnancy or labour. Sylvia was becoming more familiar and skilled at this procedure and when she was able, was thrilled to be able to feel the position of a little round, hard head through the soft tissues of a woman's abdomen, or to feel very distinctive kicks as she tried to discover in what position the baby was lying and the more difficult data of how deeply engaged in the mother's pelvis was the baby's head, or bottom if it was a breech presentation.

Sylvia was standing by an examination couch, busy clearing off and replacing the used paper towel that was attached to the bottom of each couch. It was torn off after each use and a fresh piece pulled out to cover the couch surface.

The door to the changing-room opened and the next patient to be seen entered. She looked to Sylvia to be really young but was in reality in her early twenties. Rail thin, dark complexion, a tangle of dark brown curly hair, dressed in a mismatch of clothing and a plethora of ethnic jewellery that jangled as she moved. Sylvia helped her upon the examination couch, took her urine sample bottle for it to be tested, and opened up her set of notes. She noted that this lady came from a group of gypsy travellers who had just arrived in the city and that so far she had had no antenatal care at all. The sister in charge of the antenatal clinic popped her head around the curtained screening at the same time as the legendary tutor Mrs O'Neil arrived to put the students through their paces.

Sylvia felt nervous as she performed an abdominal examination under the eagle eye of Mrs O'Neil.

All went well until she tried to find out what the presenting part of baby was. Was it a head or a bottom that was sitting in the lowest part of the lady's womb? She had prided herself on becoming quite accurate in determining the correct presentation and was disappointed in herself that on this day, of all days, in front of the senior Midwifery tutor, she just didn't know. Her hands gently palpated the woman's abdomen, searching for a little hard bony head, or a softer, wider, mass that would be indicative of a bottom. This lady was twenty-seven weeks pregnant and usually it was not too difficult to work out how the baby was lying inside the uterus.

"I'm sorry, Mrs O'Neil, I just don't know what this presentation is," said Sylvia, flushing red with embarrassment. She stepped back so that Mrs O'Neil could examine the lady herself and help Sylvia to understand more fully what she was feeling. As Mrs O'Neil expertly slid her hands around the lady's pregnant abdomen, Sylvia noticed a sudden stillness in her demeanour. She gently removed her hands, helped the lady to sit up, and said gently, "I think we need to do an X-ray to determine how your little one is lying, so if you put on the examination gown in your cubicle, Nurse Ayres will take you round to X-ray. Sylvia was surprised that even Mrs O'Neil wasn't sure how baby was lying and it made her feel not so down-hearted that she couldn't discern the presentation of baby either.

Mrs O'Neil went down the corridor to speak to Sister in charge and get an X-ray request form signed by a doctor whilst Sylvia waited for the lady to get changed so that she could escort her just around the corner to the X-ray department, which was sited conveniently in the antenatal clinic itself.

After depositing her patient, Sylvia went back to the clinic and was then sent on a much-needed coffee break. She pushed open the coffee room door in the basement and found her friend Rosie Smith in there and Penny too. She recounted her experience that even the legendary Mrs O'Neil had not known, which must surely be a first they surmised. All too soon they were back on their feet, heading for their respective ward areas and Sylvia was really looking forward to seeing the result of the X-ray that would determine what she and Mrs O'Neil had not.

She walked through the swing doors that took her to the cubicle examination area and almost bumped into the group of clinicians standing there. The

Consult Obstetrician, Senior Registrar, Sister in charge, and Mrs O'Neil were all huddled in a group, very quietly talking and looking at an X-ray that was being held up to the light. They all decamped into the doctor's office, closed the door, and Sylvia could see through the glass partition that intense discussion was taking place. Their expressions were serious, and Sylvia realised immediately that there was a problem.

It was more than an hour later before Sister came and sought Sylvia out to update her on what had happened. She brought the lady's notes with her and took Sylvia into an empty cubicle to discuss the results of the X-ray and the lady's continuing care. She turned on the X-ray viewer positioned on the wall, and slid the X-ray into it, illuminating the detail.

Sylvia could see immediately that something was not right. Baby's spine and limbs were clearly visible, but the head shape was so poorly defined that she had difficulty seeing it at all. Sister carefully explained that baby was abnormally developed in the head area. The whole vault of the skull, the large bony section at the back, had failed to develop, and parts of the interior brain mass were exposed. Baby also had very severe spina bifida, which apparently was quite common with this condition that was known as Anencephaly.

She rapidly realised that Mrs O'Neil had known straight away what she was feeling but had sensitively and calmly organised tests in a way that had not immediately panicked mum.

Sylvia was stunned at what she saw on the X-ray. This was her first experience of any abnormality. So far she had been sheltered from any such cases as her first year of experiences concentrated on the normal, with the premise that really knowing the normal well would equip her to recognise when something that was not normal presented itself. In fact, that was exactly what had happened to her that morning. She hadn't known what it was, but she knew something was not right.

She had so many questions to ask and the answers she received upset her more than she thought possible.

Sister went on to explain that this condition was incompatible with living a separate life.

"But this baby is alive, I felt it moving and kicking," she exclaimed. Sister patiently explained that this was only so because baby was not relying on its own respiratory system, as the placenta was performing the job of providing oxygen. As soon as baby was born, the respiratory centres in the brain would normally take over but this would not be possible as these areas of baby's brain were missing. Normally, she explained, these babies were stillborn, having died during pregnancy, and most died during labour or very shortly afterwards.

Sylvia was heartbroken, for the mother, for baby, for herself, and for the cruel twist of fate that determined that this baby's only taste of life would be limited to the time spent inside his or her mother's womb.

"What will happen now?" she asked.

"The results and what they mean for her baby have been discussed with the mother and her husband and they have a huge decision to make. As you know they must be able to make an informed consent so it's really important that they have access to all the information that it's possible to have. Up to twenty-eight weeks, as the law states, she can have an abortion and have the pregnancy terminated if she so wishes. Or she can choose to continue with her pregnancy, knowing what the inevitable outcome will be." Sylvia tried to imagine what the mother must have been feeling, and just couldn't, it was so awful to even think about, let alone have to experience the consequences of her decision.

She contemplated long and hard over the next few

days about the Midwives' role of having to tell, discuss the stark cruel facts, and then support the woman in labour, knowing that she must manage her own emotions and morale stance as well as supporting the woman and her husband. And how on earth did she, when qualified, support the parents at the actual moment of birth, knowing that a baby with possibly multiple abnormalities might or might not be alive after all the pushing and hard labour was done? The words 'hard labour' took on a new meaning in Sylvia's eyes.

"Never," she thought, "has a truer word been spoken."

It was that experience on the antenatal clinic that was the beginning of her understanding of the true nature and breadth of the profession that she had chosen to embrace. Mostly, and certainly in the public's eyes, birth was all about life, a joyous occasion to be celebrated, and usually it was. But there were other responsibilities, as Sylvia was learning, that were just as crucial. Supporting parents during times when their babies were not going to survive and being with them was equally important. It was a life-changing time for Sylvia, a time of great personal growth, of maturing quickly beyond her years. Having to support and manage deeply traumatised and distressed parents did that to you, she mused. It made you question what life was all about, what was it for? It was all a big lottery, she had decided, and there but for the grace of God goes any of us. What mattered in the moment was what you did and said to support any parents who had the great tragedy to lose a child. They would never, ever forget what was said or done as they experienced an event that would stand out as the most traumatic of their lives. Those events also stayed within Sylvia's memories too, and they underlined even more, if that was possible, the beautiful sanctity of life and how very precious it was. The journeys and outcomes of each woman's pregnancy were as varied as stars in the sky, each one unique with a beginning and an end. She couldn't always change outcomes and give women what they craved the most. But she could travel through that journey with them, hold their hand, and give them some of her strength to get them through the many trials that women throughout the ages and into the future would have to bear throughout their childbearing years.

Chapter Nine

In the second year of her training, Sylvia and all the other students in her set would be expected to live away from home for three months in a house situated on a council estate in the city where they were to be continually on call from Monday morning until Friday evening. They would participate in antenatal clinics, parent craft classes, and post-natal care, as well as attending home births in order to gain some community experience. They were allowed home for the weekend but needed to be back early to return to work promptly each Monday morning. A housekeeper kept the house clean and provided lunch and tea if, by some miracle, they were there to eat it. If any home births were due, as soon as labour started the students were contacted by the Midwife on call for that night and they were expected to attend cases with her and take on the care and delivery of the baby, taking more and more responsibility as their training progressed.

It was in such a community setting on a Friday afternoon, as the light was beginning to fade, that Sylvia could be found pounding on the door in front of her for the third time. The antenatal clinic at the hospital had requested a visit to a patient who frequently did not attend for her antenatal care visits. It was about five o'clock and the last visit of the day was on a notorious council estate in the south of the city. Rows of dilapidated terraced and semi-detached houses built at the turn of the century were crammed together in such a cramped layout that the sun never managed to warm their grimy façade.

Sylvia stood next to Gwyneth, an experienced midwife who had worked in such environments for years. She had told her tales that had made her squirm, laugh out loud, and cry in equal measure. Gwyneth was small in stature with short dark hair, warm brown eyes, and such a non-judgemental persona that even the most difficult families succumbed to her motherly, caring nature. She mothered everyone in the truest sense of the word and loved her job so much she often said she would have done it without being paid. And those who knew her well knew it was true. As they stood waiting at the door, they both knew the lady they had come to visit was in because they had seen the curtain twitch in the front window as they had navigated a selection of child's scooters, bikes, discarded wellingtons, and an old pram as they carefully negotiated the narrow path at the front of the house to get to the front door. They had been given this home visit to do because other colleagues had tried unsuccessfully to gain access to carry out an antenatal check. This lady was pregnant, unbelievably (to Sylvia) for the thirteenth time and had some complications but she kept missing her antenatal appointments on a regular basis. Sylvia looked around at the debris scattered across the front garden path and it reminded her of a picture she had seen once of a derelict abandoned bomb site, craters of dug-up earth intermingled with a mountain of sand-pit tools, and an old fridge, rusting away up by the hedge whose door hung on by one hinge.

Inside the house, Phyllis sat back on the battered settee, dragged her aching feet up onto the stool, and pulled the packet of cigarettes out of her worn, woollen cardigan. She contemplated the pile of dirty dishes piled high in the sink, lit a very crushed cigarette, inhaled deeply as she did so and blew smoke rings into a room that was already hazy from the other two smokers. There was more banging on the front door that Phyllis and everyone else in the room ignored, until it was repeated twice again.

"Get that, Eric, will you, love, my feet are killing me," and Phyllis wriggled deeper into the settee, trying to ease the ache that had started in her back. Eric, Phyllis's husband, peaked through a grimy lace curtain at the window and said,

"It's them again, those midwives, only there's two of 'em this time."

Phyllis sighed, stubbed the cigarette out on the fire grate she was sitting by, and pulled herself off the settee with great effort, as her considerable girth and advanced pregnancy rendered physical activity to almost zero.

"Let them in, we'll have no peace till we do."

Eric pulled the door open wide as dusk was falling outside, and he invited the two midwives into the living-room cum kitchen area.

Sylvia, sporting a navy-blue gabardine mackintosh and a pill box hat to match, which was the then student midwife's community uniform, was still mesmerised by not only the complexity of the cases she was learning about, but by the characters who inhabited the bodies that she examined on a daily basis. She stood in the front room cum kitchen and watched as Gwyneth introduced herself and prepared to carry out a full antenatal check on the very pregnant lady in front of her. She had missed three check-ups in a row and her numerous previous pregnancies and obstetric history labelled her as a high-risk case for developing complications.

This was why they had arrived late on a Friday afternoon, hoping to catch Phyllis in, as other midwives had failed to gain entrance to the house on previous visits. Sylvia was beginning to be not so judgmental, as she became more and more immersed in the lives of the women she was helping to care for. Often, women who defaulted their care had such a barrage of other problems to contend with, like violent husbands, or poverty the likes of which she had never seen before, she soon realised she had no right to be in any way disapproving and doubted she would have coped half as well as most of them seemed to. It was a sobering experience to discover just how very difficult the lives were for some of the women she cared for.

The room they stood in was dominated by a television in the corner. It was turned on and the volume was so loud that normal conversation was almost impossible. Gwyneth, with a smile, quietly asked for the volume to be lowered a little and guided Phyllis to the settee, which was covered in a jumble of coats, cushions, and empty crisp packets. Phyllis almost flattened the family's pet cat with her bulk as she lowered herself down onto the jumble of cushions. It had crawled under one of the coats and was only visible by the tip of a striped ginger tail. Swishing, it jumped down from the settee and immediately relocated itself onto the chair Sylvia had just vacated. Sylvia waited for Gwyneth to finish examining Phyllis and she was then allowed to carry out an abdominal examination under Gwyneth's watchful eye. It was a very different experience working in a community setting. There were no sterile surfaces, no hospital beds that could be adjusted to a height that saved stress to the professional's back. Sylvia kneeled down onto the carpet that was threadbare and badly in need of a good hovering and was grateful for the small protection that her black wooden tights gave to her knees.

Because Phyllis had borne so many children her abdominal muscles were very lax as they had been stretched so many times throughout her multiple pregnancies. It made the procedure of trying to discern in what position the baby was lying so much easier. It also had a downside. Sometimes this lack of abdominal tone allowed babies to lie in very unfavourable positions for delivery and that created huge problems at delivery time. A baby could be found to be lying straight across inside the uterus in a transverse position and not head down. If the baby stayed in this position and labour started, it would be impossible to deliver the baby vaginally and if not diagnosed could result in a prolonged labour and a ruptured uterus, a potentially lethal outcome for mother and baby. Fortunately, Phyllis's baby was not lying in a transverse position; it was a longitudinal lie, with baby's head deeply tucked down into the pelvic cavity. Sylvia finished Phyllis's examination by placing a black plastic pinards stethoscope onto her abdomen and managed to find the baby's heartbeat quite easily. She was becoming much more adept at this, though she still struggled on a few. Her ears had become over the last year much more attuned to hearing that very distinctive sound of a foetal heartbeat. As Gwyneth finished writing on the patient's record card and Sylvia helped Phyllis up from the settee, she glanced out of the window onto the darkening street outside and frowned. In the gathering gloom just outside the gate on the road was a tall, burly man, wearing a worn, well-patched jacket, flat cap, and with what looked like a full-grown dead sheep slung carelessly around his shoulders, like a designer scarf. She knew it was dead because its head swung from side to side as the man walked and the sheep's eyes were glassy and unseeing.

She was so astounded that her mouth fell open and she couldn't get the words out without a struggle.

"Phyllis there's a man with a dead sheep standing outside your gate!"

"Yes, that's right, love, he comes every Friday night, pops over the back fields for us, and provides the joints. Farmer hasn't caught him yet, 'ad some near misses though," and she put back her head and roared with laughter. Phyllis's husband had the grace to look slightly abashed and quietly slunk into the adjoining kitchen section of the living-room.

"Well, I've seen it all now," mused Sylvia as they left the council house, carefully skirting the obstacle course up the path again to the relative safety of the pavement. Phyllis stood at the front door, valiantly promising to cut down on her smoking as her husband passed over another cigarette.

Chapter Ten

Sylvia was awoken by the alarm clock, its tinny reverberations making it clatter across the wooden bedside cabinet. She groped across in the darkness to find the switch to the bedside light and blinked in the ensuing brightness. A cold winter's morning had resulted in frost-rhymed windows and she could hear the stirring of early traffic outside. It was still quite early, six o'clock, but she wanted to get into the bathroom before the other student Midwives awoke. The live-in house that had become home from Monday through till Friday for three months in the second year of their training was still slumbering. In another hour or so, Marge, one of the housekeepers, would be arriving to cook their breakfast and prepare lunch and tea.

Shivering, she climbed out of bed and opened the door onto the corridor where she noted that the other four doors were closed. They had been here for six weeks now and were learning how different it was to practise Midwifery in a community setting. Each of the students was attached to an experienced community Midwife. Every day the students would accompany their Midwife on her antenatal and postnatal visits and attend the clinics that she ran. When her Midwife deemed her sufficiently competent, she was given confidence cases whereby she would go alone to visit patients and carry out all of the checks needed on mother and baby. The hardest bit was being on call all night, every night for the four nights a week that they were in residence. Being on call meant attending any emergency call-outs and attending any home births that were booked by the mentor Midwife. If the student was short on deliveries other Midwives could call them out as well. Already, Sylvia had experienced numerous occasions where she had worked all day, crawled into bed dog-tired, only to be awoken by the telephone a scant few hours later informing her that another mother booked for a home birth was in labour.

Last night had been one of the few where the phone had not rung and all of the students had been grateful for badly needed extra hours sleep. Sylvia entered the bathroom, reached for the shower cubicle doors, and never got to turn the faucet on as the noise of the phone ringing reached her ears. Hurrying down the stairs she grabbed the receiver and reached for the pen and notepad that she knew would be needed. It was Gwyneth who she had worked with before. She was not Sylvia's own community Midwife, but she had a home birth that was due any day now and all the students were fighting to get as many deliveries as they could. All students were required to carry out certain numbers of deliveries to satisfy the Central Midwives' board who dictated what their training requirements were.

Fulfilling as many deliveries as possible, students were grateful for any they could get. Sylvia and her set had gone beyond the stage where they were just witnessing deliveries for their record books. With a year and a half of tuition and hands-on experience under their belts, they were now, under the eagle eyes of their mentor Midwives, actually being allowed to deliver babies, still under supervision, providing they had passed all the previous criteria that their training dictated.

Gwyneth had met Sylvia again only a few days earlier when a community staff meeting had been held at a local clinic. Here a worrying case was discussed in detail. This same mother, who had gone into labour, was the case that had been discussed.

Gwyneth had spent some time sharing her concerns about this family who had only recently arrived in the city. They had moved frequently from city to city, had a couple of very young children and were not very welcoming when home visits were made. They lived on a notorious council estate where even the police would only make home visits in twos. The community Midwifery manager presiding over a planning meeting expressed deep concern about the safety of her Midwifery colleagues when a family was known to be aggressive, either physically or verbally, and had issued instructions that they were not to visit alone to such houses. If these concerns arose, the Midwife alerted the hospital manager to where they were visiting in case any extra back-up was needed as well as alerting another on-call Midwife to attend the house with them.

Sylvia showered and dressed in record time and grabbed her delivery bag from the storeroom, forcing down a piece of toast and ruefully smelling the cooked breakfast that the other students would be able to enjoy. Dawn was breaking as she turned her car into the road of one of the most notorious council estates in the city. She pulled up outside the only house with a light on and grabbed her delivery nursing bag that had been issued along with the community outdoor uniform a few weeks earlier. Confident as she was about her growing knowledge and ability, she could not envisage anytime soon when she would have the skills to be able to manage the situation that was now in progress behind the door in front of her. A lot of her fellow students, especially those who had no community experience yet, thought that the high tension, gut-rolling drama of the Labour Ward with lots of handsome young medical interns around every corner was definitely the place to be once they had qualified, but Sylvia was beginning to recognize the very different skill sets that were needed to be working mostly alone without a team of skilled professionals next door to call upon.

Gwyneth opened the door to let Sylvia in and she followed her into a very dark living-room lit only by a few candles and a lamp base without a shade on it. Tina was lying on a battered settee, her husband nowhere to be seen. Gwyneth still had her coat on and was busy opening her antenatal bag and trying to make a space on the coffee table to put her equipment.

It was obvious even to Sylvia's inexperienced eyes that the lady in front of her was well on in labour. Strong, frequent contractions rendered conversation almost impossible and there was a distinctly wet patch underneath where Tina was sitting, indicating that the bag of waters around her baby had ruptured and delivery could be imminent. Sylvia knew she had two other young children from the detail presented at the meeting to discuss her case, and she presumed they were in bed upstairs.

There was a strange smell in the living-room that Sylvia couldn't place which pervaded everything. It wasn't a scented candle, in fact the space she was standing in would have benefitted enormously from one. The room was furnished with a mishmash of furniture, most looking long past its best. The curtains were grubby and there were tobacco stains on the ceiling. The window had an old white sheet tacked up to the window frame with a few nails. There was no carpet on the floor, just worn, red quarry tiles.

Gwyneth knelt down at the side of the settee and placed a hand onto Tina's abdomen as she experienced another strong, powerful contraction. Tina grabbed for the Entonox mask that was attached to a cylinder of oxygen and nitrous oxide, commonly known as laughing gas, that Gwyneth had brought to the house along with other equipment. This was the standard pain relief offered to labouring women in the early stages of labour. She breathed long and hard through the mask over her nose and mouth as the contraction reached its peak.

"Nurse Ayres, just pass me that pinards, will you, so I can listen into baby."

Tina had fallen back onto the settee as her contraction diminished in strength, the mask falling from her face as she did so. She had a very satisfied-like smile on her face, a dreamy expression quite unlike any other labouring woman's face at that stage of labour that Sylvia had seen so far. From her own observations, women in labour, just prior to the pushing stage, mostly reacted in a similar way. They reached the end of their tether, swore, said they couldn't go on any longer, and then, almost as if their bodies knew what their limitations were, they wanted to push and the very act of pushing and being active in the process seemed to give them back some modicum of control. Tina opened her eyes and looked at the gentle, quietly spoken Midwife who was examining her.

"It's good stuff, Sister, better than what you got there."

She slurred, and almost nodded off, which to Sylvia's eyes was remarkable considering the length and strength of the contractions that were coming thick and fast now, every two or three minutes in a relentless onslaught.

Gwyneth's expert hands located the position of baby's back and placed the pinards in the spot most likely to pick up the baby's heartbeat. She listened intently and then repeated the process three times, each time spending longer and listening more intently. She caught Sylvia's eyes looking at her strangely, and she gave an almost imperceptible negative shake of her head, her face grave with worry. Tina was still flat out in between contractions, as if she had been given a powerful sedative, which Sylvia found mystifying. Leaning forward, Gwyneth gently shook Tina awake.

"Tina, what have you taken, my love? Can you tell me?" she said as Tina grabbed for the Entonox mask again. A few minutes later, after the contraction subsided, Tina opened her eyes again and smiled at Gwyneth and Sylvia.

"Just a bit of whacky backy, love. Started it yesterday when the pains come."

Gwyneth stood up and said, "Where's your sink, Tina?"

Tina waved a hand towards a door.

"Through there, love, through there," she said dreamily.

Sylvia gave her the Entonox mask to hold as another contraction reduced Tina to a gasping, panting hulk.

She followed Gwyneth into the tiny kitchen space where she was amazed to see row upon row of green plants, covering every available bit of free space. They were on the sink, in the sink, on the windowsill, and rows three deep covered most of the kitchen floor. The heat hit her like a warm wave, coming from a number of plugged-in electric heaters.

"She's been self-medicating with home-grown cannabis since she went into labour, and I can't find a heartbeat," said Gwyneth. "We are going to have to take her into hospital. I will need to go and find a phone, as she's progressing quite quickly and we need an ambulance now."

She went back into the living-room, followed closely by Sylvia.

"Where are the two little ones?" asked Gwyneth.

A dreamy response from Tina informed them that the children were upstairs in bed. Gwyneth opened a vaginal examination pack onto the grubby coffee table next to the settee and perched precariously on the end. She carried out an internal examination to verify how far on in labour Tina was.

Six centimetres and a very thin cervix and very definitely a breech presentation. She could feel the baby's bottom very clearly.

There was no way that Gwyneth wanted an undiagnosed breech birth at home, notwithstanding the fact that so far she had not been able to detect any signs of life in this full-term baby. Breech births presented many problems that a headfirst delivery did not. The largest part of a baby that needed to pass through the bony birth canal was baby's head. If that came through, then the rest of the relative soft tissues of the body would nearly always easily follow unless there was a compound presentation where an arm or hand was also tucked close to the side of baby's head. With a breech presentation, the head comes out last and if there are difficulties for whatever reason at this stage there is only a window of about four minutes to deliver baby, as the cord providing lifesaving oxygen to baby is compressed between the hard bony head and the side walls of the bony pelvis as the head rotates through the pelvis on its final stage of delivery.

Gwyneth realized how serious this situation was. Three houses up had a phone she knew, as she had recently looked after the family with another pregnancy, and she hoped desperately that they would let her use it. One of the great advantages of working in a specified geographical patch for years was that Midwives got to know the families very well indeed, and vice versa. Often, after delivering numerous babies to the same mum and family, a great rapport and reciprocal fondness developed. There was also an unwritten code that protected well-known community figures like Midwives and Doctors that gave them a much-needed sense of security even though it was little use at three a.m., alone with just a torch when trying to find an address on an emergency callout.

Leaving Sylvia to carry on supporting Tina with the administration of Entonox, Gwyneth went and banged on the door up the street three doors away, waking the whole family up. She was never so grateful again as she was then to find the experienced older mother who understood Gwyneth's need to ring the hospital for help and gave her free access to the only phone in the street.

She contacted the Labour Ward and informed them of the situation, instructing them that she had an emergency and to send an ambulance as soon as possible. She also needed the help of social services as Tina did not know where her husband was and there were two young children who needed to be taken care of. The Labour Ward suite manager said she would contact the emergency on-call social worker and ask them to get out to the house as a matter of great urgency.

On returning to Tina's house, she discovered that the two toddlers asleep upstairs had awoken and come downstairs. Sylvia had tucked them both into the armchair next to the settee and covered them with a couple of coats she had found hanging on the back of a door. Two sets of large brown eyes, above which were heads supporting masses of blonde curly hair, turned towards her as she came back through the front door and into the living-room. They both scrutinized her quietly and seemed completely unfazed by the fact that two strangers were in their house in the early morning. They sat without moving, showing no signs of distress, even when Tina started to moan, cry out, and breathe with desperation into the Entonox mask that she was gripping tightly to her face.

Tina finished breathing through a very strong contraction holding the Entonox mask so closely to her face that when she removed it as the contraction faded away an imprint of the mask was left behind.

Gwyneth knew she had an uphill task now, as she had to try and persuade Tina to accept the fact that she needed to go to the hospital. She sat down next to her and took her hand. This was going to be difficult. Another contraction assaulted Tina before Gwyneth could say another word; the contractions were longer and stronger now.

Sylvia and Gwyneth manoeuvered Tina into a sitting position on the settee with great difficulty, and Sylvia marvelled at the tender, calming way that Gwyneth explained that her baby needed to be in hospital for delivery. Fortunately, Tina was so high on the substances that she had smoked that she put up no resistance at all, just grabbing hold of the Entonox mask with each contraction, breathing deeply and then becoming semi-comatose in between. She asked no questions, even when Gwyneth told her that some ladies from social services were coming along to take care of her little ones until they could find her husband.

Lights from outside illuminated the front window and an engine could be heard as a vehicle pulled up. Gwyneth and Sylvia both breathed an enormous sigh of relief as they realized that the ambulance had arrived. They had come on a blue light, tyres screaming all the way, arriving in record time. They trundled down the path at the front of the house pushing a wheelchair, shouting out a hearty greeting as they stepped into the very crowded living-room. Sylvia went over and sat with the two toddlers, sitting on the easy chair up the corner. Their eyes were wide, faces solemn, and still no sound emitted from them, no cries out for mum or dad.

As Gwyneth explained the urgency and need to get the labouring lady in front of them to the hospital as fast as possible to the ambulance staff, Sylvia heard a noise in the back kitchen and the door was flung open with such force that it caused it to hit and then bounce back of the wall it was attached to.

"What the fuck is going on – what you doin' in my house?" shouted Tina's husband. "And where do you think you are taking her?"

Sylvia noticed that both the toddlers shrank back and were utterly still, their eyes not leaving him, looking very afraid. She also felt quite afraid of the burly aggressive man who glowered at both Gwyneth and her.

Mick Travis was a big man; dirty, unkempt long hair, unshaven, and a bellow on him that many a police officer in the not-too-recent past had been in the presence of. He'd spent the night sleeping off a massive hangover on a park bench and he still stank of alcohol.

Sylvia was so petrified of him she realized she was shaking. The anger flowed from him in waves, and she stepped back from the chair, almost tripping over the cat as she did so.

"Mr Travis, we need to take your wife to hospital,"

said Gwyneth, quite firmly. "There may be some problems with baby and there is no way we can look after mum and baby here. She must go in, now."

Mick Travis ignored Gwyneth and made a lunge for his wife who was in the process of being lifted into the wheelchair by the two male ambulance attendants.

"Get the fuck out of my house, she's going nowhere," he snarled. He almost tipped the chair over and his wife with it, knocking the ambulance driver onto the floor in the process. Sylvia looked at him and his widely dilated pupils, almost retching at the stale, acrid smell of alcohol that still emanated from him.

As the now irate ambulance driver got to his feet, there was more commotion at the front door. Social services had arrived in the guise of two women. There was now a total of seven adults and two toddlers in the living-room making the verbal confrontation seem even more intense and chaotic. Sylvia watched as an incredibly calm Gwyneth repeated her request and informed Mick Travis that he could come with his wife to hospital, that social services would care for the children in his absence and if he did not agree and let them transport his wife in, she would have to call the police.

The mention of the word police seemed to do the trick, and Sylvia realized that Gwyneth knew that no way would Mick Travis want the police in his house in view of what was growing in pots in the kitchen, and his own obvious drug use. Still swearing and threatening everyone in the room, he very begrudgingly allowed the ambulance staff to load Tina back into the wheelchair and into the back of the ambulance.

A crowd had gathered by this time and lights were on in every house in the street. The two ladies from social services said they would stay with the children and set up short-term care if it was needed. Gwyneth climbed into the back of the ambulance with Tina, telling Sylvia to follow in her own car. Travis, still swearing, said he would drive his own battered vehicle to the hospital and he would see them there, which Gwyneth doubted.

Sylvia was still shaking from shock as she climbed into her little Mini, and valiantly tried to keep up with the ambulance, which had its siren and blue lights flashing all the way to the hospital. She soon lost sight of it as it jumped red lights and broke the legal speed limit to get mother and baby into hospital as soon as possible.

Inside the ambulance, Gwyneth was on her knees by the side of Tina who was securely strapped into the ambulance trolley. Tina was wanting to push with each contraction now, an undiagnosed breech presentation pushing down hard with each contraction, a baby demanding to make his entrance into the world.

Gwyneth talked Tina through each contraction calming, soothing, encouraging use of the Entonox to try and stop Tina from pushing. Four miles to the hospital had never seemed so tortuous. She knew how disastrous this delivery could become if baby was going to be born bottom first, apart from the terrible possibility that this baby had already died inside the uterus hours ago. Her knees were bruised from the battering of trying to stay upright on the ambulance floor, and as they took corners on two wheels often, the other member of ambulance staff tried valiantly to keep her upright as she cajoled, advised, and comforted Tina who by now was making deep guttural sounds in her throat which Gwyneth knew announced the start of the second stage of labour, the pushing stage.

"How much longer now?" she shouted to the driver. "She's wanting to push."

"Nearly there, love, nearly there."

Seconds later she heard a screech of brakes. All motion stopped and the back doors of the ambulance were flung open to the marvellous sight of two senior labour suite Midwives and a registrar.

"You don't do things by halves, Colclough, do you!" quipped one of Gwyneth's colleagues, as they expertly in super-fast time loaded Tina onto their waiting trolley and headed for the Labour Ward with Gwyneth following behind.

Sylvia arrived ten minutes later, and she dashed down the corridor to find Gwyneth who was at the nurse station at the entrance to the Labour Ward.

"They have taken her into theatre for the delivery just in case baby gets stuck and a Cesarean is needed," said Gwyneth.

"What about baby's heartbeat?" said Sylvia.

"I don't know yet, all I know is that I couldn't find it on examination," said Gwyneth sadly.

They settled themselves into the staff sitting-room and Gwyneth went through the details of the morning's events with Sylvia. They were still sitting there with much-needed tea and toast provided by Mercy from the kitchen when the Registrar came out of the theatre and sat down next to them. The look on his face told them both what they didn't want to know, that the child, an eight-pound baby-boy with no obvious abnormalities had been born showing no signs of life. He explained to Sylvia that sometimes this happened, that an apparently healthy baby, showing no problems at all for nine months in the womb, could suddenly die a few short hours before birth. If mum had been in hospital from early labour, then any foetal distress could have been picked up, but because this event had occurred before the Midwife had arrived there was little they could have done which would have changed the outcome. It seemed from examination of baby that he had died inside the womb only very recently and not weeks ago.

The Registrar asked where the father of the baby was. It was now over an hour since they had arrived at the hospital and there was no sign of him.

He finally arrived at lunch time, five hours later, very drunk and swearing at any staff he came into contact with. He showed no remorse for his behaviour, no sorrow for the death of his baby, just an all-consuming anger that it was the hospital's fault and he was suing for neglect. He didn't want to see his son and swore at his wife for allowing 'the social services' into their house. He threatened 'to get those two' who came to his house, meaning the Midwives, and said he had taken their car registrations. Nothing came of the threat but it worried Sylvia a lot at the time.

The whole episode had a profound impact on her. That last year of her training, she felt that she had grown up. The multi-tangled webs of people's lives that inexorably impacted on their child-bearing years and the problems they presented with resulted in scenarios that Sylvia thought would not have been believed by herself just twelve months ago. Her working days could be marvellous, beautiful, and life-affirming. Or they could be traumatic, devastating, and terrible, leaving her wondering if there was a god, any god who cared, when she saw women desperate for a child suffer their fifth miscarriage in a row and then, in the antenatal clinic, listen to women asking for a termination of pregnancy, their third in a row, especially when a termination could take place up to twenty-eight weeks of pregnancy. Some of those babies were born alive and it was devastating for staff to witness this as they waited for the inevitable demise of a baby's life in a profession where saving and preserving life were normally paramount.

She slowly came to terms with the fact that she couldn't solve everyone's problems, that some people rejected help when offered. Sometimes no matter how hard she and others tried, babies would die and that no amount of help or expertise would have changed the outcome in some of the cases she was involved in.

Chapter Eleven

It was visiting time on the general practitioner unit on the sixth floor of the maternity unit. It was Christmas Eve and snowing hard, the snow being hurled against the large plate glass windows that covered most of the building by a brisk wind. Sylvia was working there to try and get some more deliveries. Her training would not be complete unless she had performed the requisite number of at least forty births and documented and got them signed off by her mentor Midwife.

She liked working on the GP unit, as it was usually known, as all the cases were low risk, nice and normal, and once delivered, the mums and babies stayed on that ward for a few days, care being shared between General Practitioners and the Midwives. The women came in from home, in labour, accompanied by their husbands or boyfriends. If labour was in the early stages, women were encouraged to be mobile, to walk up and down the ward if they wanted to. It was a lovely, relaxed mix of delivering babies, helping with breastfeeding or bottle-feeding problems, showing new mums how to bathe their babies, and giving good parenting advice.

Sylvia had been in the nursery room at one end of the ward, bottle-feeding a very hungry baby whose mum was feeling exhausted from a long labour. It was also an excuse for cuddle time with the new-borns. Recently delivered babies had a very distinct smell before they had their first bath. Maybe it was the liquor amnii, the fluid inside the womb that babies are surrounded by until birth. It was a smell, definitely not unpleasant, but it was like a tantalising subliminal message that whispered to Sylvia. It said, 'Hold me close, tuck me in under your chin, rest your velvet-like cheek against mine, let me feel you relax as your baby breaths become regular.' When babies went to sleep, welded in place it seemed to her neck, their skin to her skin, snuggled up and dreaming their secret dreams, as she knew babies did, it was like a litany of sorts that put her into a place of the deepest contentment and satisfaction. The harsher realities of Midwifery practice faded for a short time as she breathed in their special scent and marvelled at their perfectness. Somehow their breathing and hers would become almost synchronised and for a little while nothing else mattered.

Her little moments of pure delight with her babies in the nursery usually didn't last for long. The door was pushed open and Caddy, a state-enrolled nurse who worked usually on the antenatal clinic but helped out in other areas when the unit was busy, called out to her.

"Are you after some more deliveries, Nurse Ayres? There's a lady down the other end getting on and Sister Hussey says to get yourself down there."

Needing no more encouragement, Sylvia expertly winded the baby she was holding and was rewarded with a robust burp. She wrapped her little charge in a clean cotton wrap, planted a loving kiss on her downy head, and tucked her back into the Perspex cot on wheels that all the babies in the maternity hospital were nursed in. She marched swiftly down the other end of the corridor where the two labour rooms were situated and entered the one that showed signs of activity. Sister Hussey was a motherly, caring, rotund, sensible woman who all the students loved working with. Calm, and with a 'can do' attitude, the mothers loved her too. She could work wonders with women who were tired and at the end of their tether, who thought they couldn't cope any longer with their labour. She would mother them, mobilise them, and give them back their belief in their own bodies' ability to do what nature, nine times out of ten, got right.

Sylvia could see straight away that the mum in front of her lying on the delivery bed was about to enter the second stage of labour. Her contractions were coming thick and fast one after the other with hardly any break in between. It was the lady's second baby and everything was casebook normal. The lady's name was Linda, and she breathed long and hard into the Entonox mask that she was clutching to her face. She was a confident, experienced mum whose aim in life was to nurture a large brood of children. Her husband was at home with their other child and was on his way back in, probably hampered by the snow that was piling up outside.

Sylvia was now experienced enough to set up the delivery trolley and prepare any equipment needed. She expertly opened a delivery pack, dropped a pair of sterile gloves onto the sterile inner section of the pack, and then with the help of Sister Hussey climbed into her sterile green delivery gown having first scrubbed her hands up to the elbow to within an inch of their life. She slid her hands into the gloves using the no-touch technique that she had been taught during the first few days of her training. It seemed a lifetime away now. She was no longer a gawky, scared student with no confidence in herself, but well on the way to becoming a member of a profession like no other, which, bar one, was the oldest in the world.

Linda pushed and then pushed some more. She was relieved to have reached the second stage or pushing stage as she called it. Instead of just lying there and somehow coping with those huge contractions, she could actively be doing something, and that something was pushing. And she knew that when she got to that stage that she was nearly there, her baby would be born soon. The atmosphere in the room was relaxed and Sylvia, now gowned and masked, with gloved hands, stood on Linda's right side waiting for the next contraction to make its presence known. There was a comfortable silence, punctured only by the sound of snow batting against the outside window and in the background another sound, a cacophony that started low, but slowly built.

"What's that?" said Linda from behind her Entonox mask. "I can hear music."

"It's the Sally Army band and staff singing carols on the ward," said Sister Hussey. "They do it every year going round all the wards, and the staff bring their families and children to sing the carols for the babies."

Another contraction interrupted Linda's response, and a deep guttural moan confirmed to all present that the baby was on his way out.

The pushing became compulsive now and Sylvia steadied herself as Linda placed her right foot against her hip to use as a lever point and bore down hard and long, her neck veins bulging in the supreme effort of giving birth. Half a dozen pushes later, and with a shout of triumph, Linda gave another push and her baby's head was delivered.

Sylvia immediately felt to see if the cord was around baby's neck, which it wasn't, and watched as she did each time she delivered a baby for the little spontaneous movement of baby's head as it righted itself in line with baby's shoulder position, a crucial part of the mechanism of birth.

Linda gave another push to deliver the rest of her baby just as the choir reached their end of the corridor. A beautiful seven-and-a-half-pound baby boy was delivered, pink and healthy, with the best pair of lungs, verified by his lusty cry, that Sylvia had ever heard. The strains of 'Oh Little Town of Bethlehem' could be heard right outside the labour room door.

Sylvia listened to the singing and had never been so moved in her life. The staff and families carried on singing as baby matched their singing with his cries. Linda hugged her baby to her chest and smiled through tears of joy as Sylvia clamped and cut the cord and then delivered the placenta that had fed baby for nine months.

"Let them see him," said Linda, "please, let them see him."

"Are you sure?" said Sister Hussey.

"Yes," said Linda, "very sure."

And so Sister Hussey opened the labour room door to a crowd of strangers, who stood, all with tears in their eyes as Sylvia wrapped the baby boy she had just delivered into a clean towel and took him to the door entrance.

There wasn't a dry eye in the house as the choir finally sang a last song to a mother and her baby. It was 'Away in a Manger' and how could it have been anything else? It was a moment when a mother and two Midwives took away a memory that would stay with them forever.

Chapter Twelve

During her last week on community placement, Sylvia was busy writing up in her casebook a variety of procedures that she had mastered. Her copy of the Margaret Myles' textbook was beginning to look shabby now. She had pored over its pages endlessly, riveted and mesmerised, but also fearful that she would never be able to grasp it all. It was a thick tomb of a book, one that all the students used as their 'Bible' on all matters Midwifery. There was also Bender's Obstetrics, another well-respected textbook that was on their reading list. Gwyneth, the lovely midwife who had supported her after the aftermath of the dreadful case where the baby had died during labour, was soon to have another student Midwife who had just started her training. She was the daughter of a professor who had written a textbook on Midwifery and Sylvia wondered what the responsibility of having a student whose father was as illustrious as he was must feel like.

She had arranged to meet Gwyneth in a local health centre car park, prior to starting the list of post-natal visits planned for that day. Most mums who had had a normal delivery were seen every day for ten days. If there were any problems with mum or baby, the community midwife could visit as often as she deemed necessary and this could mean two or three visits a day if there were feeding problems, parenting difficulties, or support needed with social problems. The Midwives' code of practice covered the period up to twenty-eight days after delivery and Sylvia knew that many Midwives did see a few of their patients for that length of time, especially if post-natal depression had been diagnosed.

As Sylvia's training progressed, she was given more and more responsibility but still working under the umbrella of her support Midwife. She was given post-natal confidence cases where she would go in alone to a house to carry out the examinations, and the supporting Midwife would follow her in a little while later to assess if her examination of mum and baby was accurate. This was a good way of beginning to consolidate all the theory and practical experience she had gained so far, and she began to bloom in confidence, also loving the close relationships with the families that she cared for. Having met the families early on in pregnancy, and seeing them at the hospital antenatal clinic and also on the labour ward when she was back working on the wards, she was as delighted to see them as they were her when she pulled back a curtain from around an admission bed to find a familiar, friendly face.

Gwyneth had given her three visits to attend alone, and they had arranged to meet later that morning at the community health centre to discuss them. Her first visit was to a lovely, experienced mum who had three children, a healthy baby, and no problems at all. She lived in a comfortable semi-detached house on a big estate of newer houses, not far from the health centre. She greeted Sylvia at the front door with a big hug, baby less than one year old tucked under her arm and a toddler hanging onto her dressing gown. Her husband, a cheerful soul, was cooking breakfast in the kitchen and without asking brought in a mug of tea and a plate of bacon and egg sandwiches.

"Got to keep those calories up, eh nurse, what with all those babies waiting to be delivered."

It was those small acts of kindness, offered freely and frequently by the vast majority of patients that made Midwifery so rewarding for Sylvia. As she said goodbye thirty minutes later, she mentally reminded herself to seek out the telephone number for Weight Watchers that one of her friends was attending. Many more visits like that one and she was going to need them!

Her next visit was to a little terraced house in a cul-de-sac where the houses had seen better days, and paint was peeling of the woodwork. Chunks of rendering over the brickwork had fallen off in places and weeds were growing in the debris that had collected in the guttering. This family had arrived recently from Pakistan and mum did not speak much English. Her husband worked nights with a local taxi service, and he was always in bed when any visits were made.

Sylvia clutched her community nursing bag closer and banged on the front door. She heard a slow shuffling noise and the door was opened by an elderly relative who had come to stay and support Mrs Samina Bibi. She was led into the front room and asked to sit on the settee and the relative disappeared to go and find Mrs Bibi. A door opened and Sylvia's second patient of the day stood before her.

Samina was quiet and shy, with beautiful dark skin and thick lustrous hair that hung below her waistline. She sported a number of intricate henna tattoos, delicate and becoming. She was a first-time mother and was still reeling from leaving most of her close family and relatives behind in a hot, humid homeland to come and live in, by comparison, a dark, cold country where no one understood what she was saying.

She had no extended family to show her the basics of parenting and, to make life more difficult, she spoke no English. Her marriage had been arranged for her, but she felt she was one of the lucky ones as at least her new husband was kind and caring.

Using a lot of gesticulating and pointing, which must have looked comical to an observer, Sylvia managed to communicate and carry out a full post-natal examination. She gesticulated to Samina to lie down on the settee in the room and proceeded to check that Samina's uterus was involuting back to its normal place deep inside the pelvic cavity, that her stitches were healing and that her milk-leaking breasts were comfortable. She then helped her up into a sitting position.

"Can you go and bring baby into here so I can check him over too?" said Sylvia, mimicking rocking a baby so that Samina would understand.

Samina smiled but then shook her head, laying both hands in a prayer-like stance against the side of her cheek and closing her eyes, mimicking sleep.

Sylvia tried explaining to Samina and her aunt that she still needed to check on baby even though he was fast asleep. Samina persisted in saying no, regrettably. It seemed the family had had little sleep during the last night and understandably didn't want baby disturbing again. Sylvia was torn between not waking her baby and the tired look in both the women's eyes, but she could not write truthfully in the mother's records that she had examined him, so, feeling guilty, she gesticulated as best she could and insisted that they went into the back room to bring him in for her to see.

They brought him in, in a little Moses basket, wrapped in a sheet with no blankets on. He had no knitted hat on and lay very still, with his tiny fists both curled up under his chin. He had very pink, rosy cheeks and hands and at first glance seemed like a little picture of health, that is until Sylvia touched him.

She lifted him out onto her lap and laid a finger against the curve of his cheek. It was cold, so cold, abnormally cold. He was floppy like a little rag doll and his head rolled from side to side, as she willed him to show some sign of life. Her heart missed a beat, a steel vice clutched at her abdomen and chest and for a second she was motionless. A terrible dread was only released slightly when she saw the rise and fall of his little chest, erratic, but it was there. She knew that something was terribly wrong, and help was needed immediately. Praying that dad had a phone somewhere in the house, as he was a taxi-driver, she rapidly sent Samina's aunt to get dad out of bed and find her a phone, which, thanking her lucky stars, he had on the wall in the tiny kitchen at the back of the house. With shaking fingers, she rang Gwyneth's number and almost cried with relief when she answered immediately. She told her quickly what she had found. Amazingly, Gwyneth was in the next street, visiting a patient there and seconds later she was banging on the front door.

The baby was so still that Sylvia was sure he had expired on her knee, only the erratic movements of his chest showed her he was still breathing. She asked Samina's aunt to go and find a few of baby's blankets. Gwyneth took baby from Sylvia and, sitting on the settee, swiftly removed baby's nappy and then she inserted a thermometer into his back passage, took one look at the lowest temperature she had ever seen on a living new-born, and, using her bleep she called first for an ambulance as an emergency. She then called the neonatal intensive care unit to tell them to expect a severely hypothermic baby. Sylvia stood and watched the drama taking place in front of her and was astonished when Gwyneth started to undo her navy uniform cardigan and then started to unzip the front of her uniform dress.

"Pass me baby, over here," Gwyneth instructed, and Sylvia did so, mesmerised, as Gwyneth lifted baby Bibi and tucked him inside her dress, chest to chest and zipped him in like a kangaroo in its mother's pouch. The ambulance's sirens could be heard in the background, in the cul-de-sac, as Gwyneth tried to explain that baby was very cold and needed to go to hospital to be warmed up. Mum was to accompany baby there.

Speed was of the essence, she explained, especially with a baby whose temperature was as low as baby Bibi's.

There was another banging on the front door as the ambulance crew arrived. Samina, Gwyneth, and Sylvia all climbed into the back of the ambulance and the doors clanged shut.

"Make it fast, lads," said Gwyneth to the driver, "as fast as you possibly can."

Fortunately, the house was only about two miles from the hospital site and in no time it seemed, with a screech of brakes, they were pulling up under the huge canopy that fronted the main entrance to the maternity unit. Gwyneth almost ran the last few yards through main reception, a set of double swing doors, and she arrived at the neonatal unit door where a paediatrician and neonatal nurse were waiting with a portable incubator on wheels to receive baby into their care. Sylvia, following behind with Samina, could see from the neonatal unit corridor into the first glass-fronted room where a crowd of medics and nurses had already surrounded baby Bibi and with some haste were attaching intravenous lines, oxygen mask, and skin monitors.

From realising something was wrong to arriving at the neonatal unit with baby had taken twenty-two minutes, Sylvia surmised, the adrenaline still coursing through her body. Gwyneth, she had witnessed, had drawn a huge sigh of relief and wiped a hand across her brow as she relinquished responsibility of baby to the neonatal unit staff, saying, "My word, that was a close call, I can tell you! Come on, Nurse Ayres, we are having a very well-needed and earned cup of tea!"

Writing up the events of the last hour in the baby's records, needed by the neonatal unit staff, Sylvia listened as Gwyneth explained the dangers of neonatal hypothermia or cold baby syndrome.

When a baby's body temperature dropped below thirty-five degrees Celsius, lethal physiological changes start to take place in the body. The baby's blood sugar level starts to drop, respiration starts to slow down, fitting may occur. Oedema, or retention of fluid in the body's tissues starts to develop. Babies may look incredibly healthy with bright red, rosy cheeks and extremities but when that stage is reached death is not far away unless immediate action is taken.

Sylvia began to realise how close they had been to that awful possibility and thanked her lucky stars that she had insisted she check baby over when mum hadn't wanted her to, and that Gwyneth had been so close by when she called for some help.

Both Gwyneth and Sylvia needed to retrieve their vehicles, which were both still parked outside Samina's house. Fortunately, another member of staff was only working until lunchtime and offered to drop them back in the street. Climbing back into her car, to carry on with the list of confidence case post-natal visits and feeling very satisfied with the warm praise that the neonatal unit staff had given them both for such a quick response that had undoubtedly saved baby Bibi's life, Sylvia breathed a sigh of contentment. Yes, it had been scary, yes, she still felt a bit shaky from the adrenaline that had pumped through her veins in the ambulance journey to the hospital and yes, she still had lots to learn, especially about hypothermic babies, but would she have swapped any of it for another sort of job? Never!

Chapter Thirteen

Penny was working on one of two antenatal floors in the maternity unit. They housed a few more beds than the other wards, as the large rooms at each end of the ward were not used as a nursery for the babies but were used to increase capacity for inpatients. To say it was a busy area was an understatement. Thirty-four beds, almost permanently full of pregnant women with a huge variety of problems, always kept the staff and the students on their toes. The fearsome Sister Frenchit who, during their first week of training had shown them how to properly don a pair of sterile gloves, managed this ward. Penny could still hear her admonishments ringing in her ears from that episode of criticism and from more recent encounters.

Just an hour ago she had answered the phone at the nurse station in the centre of the ward corridor. It was a dad enquiring how his wife was and asking about visiting times. Having successfully given him this information, she put the phone down, and turned to find Sister Frenchit standing right behind her.

"Nurse Jones, when speaking on the telephone to anyone, and I mean anyone, do not use the word 'OK'. It is a slang word and not professional. Do you understand me?"

And what did she say in response?

"OK, Sister Frenchit."

To which Sister Frenchit turned a shade of puce, and in sheer exasperation instructed her to go to the sluice room where a whole row of demijohns, full of ladies' twenty-four-hour urine collections, were waiting to be measured.

Penny had recently knocked over a vase full of flowers, soaking the bed sheets on which they had landed. Fortunately, it was unoccupied at the time. And only last week when making a bed she had knocked the chart holder off the end of the bed and been accused by Sister Frenchit of 'ruining hospital property'.

Although Sister Frenchit put the fear of God in her, Penny could not help but admire the superb and flawless running and management of her ward. Two demanding Consultant Obstetricians housed their patients there and some were very sick women indeed who were not only pregnant but suffered from medical problems too. A barrage of tests was requested daily, and results were received that needed urgent acting upon, some with life-and-death implications for mother, baby, or both.

Housed in those antenatal beds were pregnant diabetic mothers, women who had heart disease but were also pregnant, women who had had multiple miscarriages and in a desperate attempt to preserve a pregnancy literally went to bed for nine months, being monitored with tests every week. There were women with low-lying placentas, who could bleed heavily at any moment. A few months ago she had come on duty to pandemonium. A grade four-placenta preavia case had suddenly, without warning, started to bleed. The afterbirth was in the wrong place, so low down inside the uterus that it stopped the baby from delivering vaginally. The patient was housed in a single side room, the door open as the porters were loading the lady onto a trolley, trying to get her downstairs as quickly as possible to the theatre staff who were waiting to perform an emergency Caesarean section in an attempt to save the mother's and the baby's life.

Penny had never seen so much blood in her life. It was pooled on the floor, underneath the bed, still dripping off the sides. The crumpled sheets were soaked in blood, their folds, and ridges on the centre of the bed, mocking their attempts. The woman, who by now was on the trolley, was as white as the driven snow, so pale she looked like a porcelain doll. Penny had learned that there was a massive increase in the blood supply to all the pelvic organs during pregnancy, and that at the end of pregnancy, a mother's total blood volume had increased by fifty percent. This was why any bleeding, but especially placenta praevia cases, could be so heavy and was particularly dangerous during pregnancy. She later was told that, by some miracle, the theatre staff had saved the life of mother and baby, but had to perform a hysterectomy, the removal of the mother's uterus, in order to save her life.

Not only were there antenatal cases to be cared for but induction of labour cases were also admitted to the ward. Some women needed to have their labours artificially triggered into action when problems indicated that the baby would be safer outside the uterus rather than in it. Mothers-to-be were given an intravenous infusion with certain drugs added that helped to induce contractions, and progress of labour had to be monitored every thirty minutes with a variety of observations carried out. There could be as many as five or six women in early labour on the ward at any one time, and often they had had problematic pregnancies too, which was why they were being induced. One of the saddest and most difficult tasks that Penny had to come to terms with was when women came in for induction of labour because the baby that was growing inside them had a foetal abnormality. Terminations of pregnancy could be carried out up to twenty-eight weeks of pregnancy, and what made it even more difficult, if that was possible, was that women who chose to have a termination of pregnancy had to labour in rooms next door to women who had normal pregnancies and babies. When healthy babies were delivered, they could hear them taking their first cry in the next room as they laboured for up to twenty-four hours or more knowing that there would be no healthy baby for them to hold at the end of it.

Looking after those ladies whose babies would not be going home with them was intensely distressing to Penny and to every other student and Midwife she had met so far. The earlier the diagnosis in pregnancy of an abnormality was made, the sooner plans could be made if a woman and her family wanted a termination of their pregnancy. But of course, some women did not choose to end their pregnancy, even if there was little chance of their baby taking any breaths at birth. They chose to let nature take its course because of religious beliefs and other moral grounds, and so midwives sometimes cared for women who were carrying a baby with a genetic abnormality that was incompatible with life outside of its mother's womb.

Penny walked down the corridor towards the furthest end of the ward, musing on the dichotomy she had about Sister Frenchit, someone so severe on the outside that women and some staff were actually scared of her, and the woman whose eagle eye and experience missed nothing, and had saved mothers' and babies' lives.

As she passed one of the bathroom doors, she heard a strange noise and stopped in her tracks. It was an unfamiliar sound, deep and guttural, and she could hear a repeating metal clang in the background. Curious, she pushed the bathroom door open and was shocked at what she saw. Lying on the floor on her back was Sandra Edwards, a patient who had been on the ward a few weeks ago. She had been admitted with very high blood pressure and the obstetrician, even with high dosage of medication, was struggling to bring it down. She had become very oedematous, and her urine samples had high levels of protein. Her face had started to look puffy and her lower legs were very swollen. Her feet bulged out over the top of her slippers. She had been put on complete bed rest, except for toilet needs, and the consultant was hoping to get her past thirty-six weeks of pregnancy before inducing her, giving her baby a few extra weeks of growth inside.

Penny knew straight away what she was witnessing, an eclamptic fit caused by oedema around the mother's brain, brought on as a consequence of a very high, uncontrolled blood pressure. It was a lethal and life-threatening obstetric emergency. Penny acted instinctively, slamming her fist onto the red emergency button situated on the wall of each bathroom.

Sandra's back was arched of the floor, her teeth clenched together. She had stopped breathing and was cyanosed. The clanging noise that Penny had heard was Sandra's foot rhythmically jerking against an overturned waste bin that had tipped over as Sandra had fallen to the ground. Penny noticed there was a large wet stain on Sandra's nightie where, as the fit had escalated, Sandra had uncontrollably passed urine and wet herself.

With great difficulty Penny turned Sandra over as gently as she could, putting her into recovery position. She hoped that would stop her airways being closed off by her tongue falling to the back of her mouth. She made sure that Sandra's uncontrollable movements were not close to anything that would damage her and gently held her limbs to reduce any further potential trauma.

The bathroom door swung open and a number of staff swarmed through the door. Leading them was Sister Frenchit. Penny almost threw her arms around her in relief as Sister Frenchit barked orders out cool as a cucumber and fired verbal instructions out to her ward team. She then emergency bleeped the consultant and rang the Labour Ward co-ordinator to say they were bringing a patient down who was fitting and could they prepare a room to 'special' the patient in.

Penny stood back as the porters and a trolley arrived, and she helped Sid, a seasoned veteran of a porter who had seen it all during his fifteen years of portering, to manoeuvre the trolley into the tight space of the bathroom. Quickly, with a practised ease, they lifted Sandra onto her side on the trolley and with two qualified Midwives accompanying him, Sid headed for the lifts that would take them all down to the ground floor.

"Nurse Jones, collect the patient's belongings from

her room and take them down to the labour room. Then I want to see you in my office," said Sister Frenchit.

Penny's heart sank. She was shocked, as she had witnessed the first fit she had ever seen, and it had scared her even though she had been taught about it. She had been given some homework only the week before and written an essay on the very subject of eclampsia. She had been on a late shift the night before, not home till well after ten, slept badly, was up again at six thirty the next morning, and was feeling really exhausted. The thought of another dressing down by Sister Frenchit made her feel a bit tearful. She had tried so very, very hard to keep up, and without the support of all of the other students in her set, she doubted she would have got this far in her training. Feeling sad and dejected, she walked back down the corridor to Sandra's side room and methodically packed all of her belongings into a black plastic sack and took the lift back down to the labour ward as requested. The first person she bumped into was Sylvia. She was in the small kitchenette between the progress department and the labour ward, making tea and toast for a lady she had just delivered.

"Hey Penny, what you up to?" beamed Sylvia. She was on a complete mental high following her recent delivery of a gorgeous little African baby who had been born with a full head of tight black curly hair and the biggest brown eyes she had ever seen.

"Do you know where they've taken the lady with eclampsia, she's just come down from my ward a few minutes ago?"

"Yes, left-hand side, bottom room. The Consultant and Registrar are with her now. Do you want me to take those down for you?" said Sylvia, eyeing the bag of Sandra's belongings.

"Thanks, not as though I'm in any hurry to get back," groaned Penny.

"Why what's up?"

"Oh, just the usual. I don't think Sister Frenchit likes me at all. I'm beginning to think I'll never make it to the end of this training," and to Sylvia's surprise, her friend's eyes filled with tears.

"Hey, come on now, you're just having a bad day. Last week I was told off big style in theatre, in a room full of people, for accidentally de-sterilising myself during a Caesarean section and not noticing. I felt mortified!"

Penny blew her nose and sighed. "I suppose you're right, I'm just so bloody tired today, which doesn't help."

Just then, the labour ward manager walked past and popped her head into the kitchenette and said, "I've lost a patient's husband. Have you seen an elderly-looking gent who you think could be someone's granddad but actually is the father?"

They both shook their heads.

"We have got to carry out an emergency Caesarean section on his wife, and we can't find him to tell him. He was here a short while ago, but now he's gone missing," and with that she hurried up the corridor, looking into the other ward areas for the absent father.

"I'd better get back or I'll be in for another telling off," said Penny handing the black bag of belongings over. "I'll see you later, hopefully at coffee break."

Penny trudged back to the ward, dreading what she was about to encounter. A few minutes later, she was standing outside Sister Frenchit's office door. Pulse-racing, dry-mouthed, and stomach-churning, she knocked timidly on the door.

"Come in." She pushed the door open, wishing the floor would swallow her up, and stepped into the dragon's den.

"Close the door, Nurse Jones."

By now, she was quaking in her shoes and looked down at the floor, willing it to be over. There was a long silence.

"Never in my life," said Sister Frenchit and Penny felt the tears re-appear. "Never in my life have I seen a young student so calm and sensible, in what was a very distressing situation."

The words were uttered in a deeply admonishing tone, almost like a telling off instead of a praiseworthy comment.

Penny couldn't believe her ears. She dared to look up.

"You might make a midwife yet." Penny couldn't help it. She smiled and stuttered her thanks, not actually believing the words she was hearing.

"Now, go down to room one and check that those induction drips have not run through."

Penny dived for the door, and, turning, said, "OK, Sister Frenchit."

She closed the door quickly at the sharp intake of breath from Sister Frenchit, cursing herself inwardly for yet another slip-up and almost skipped down the corridor, breathing a deep sigh of relief and thinking, 'There is a god after all!'

Later, in the coffee room, Penny was recounting her meeting with Sister Frenchit. Sylvia was laughing as Penny admitted to the OK faux pas and swore she would never say OK ever again.

"Was the missing father found?" asked Penny.

"You'll never believe it," said Sylvia. "He was fifty something and she was only seventeen and they were distantly related! Apparently, he wandered off from the labour room to find the sitting-room in progress area, and went into the storage room of sterilised packs by mistake. He had a heart attack and collapsed and was found about five minutes later and transferred across to the city hospital next door, where he underwent major surgery whilst his wife was in theatre having a section!"

"You couldn't make it up, could you?" mused Penny, and swallowing the last dregs of a much-needed cup of coffee, she and Sylvia headed back to another shift of experiences that would continue to shape and mould them into the honourable rank of Midwife.

Chapter Fourteen

It was a bright summer's morning and the atmosphere on the labour ward was buzzing. Every bed on the ward was full. The large wipe-on-wipe-off board by the nurses' station where each room's occupant's details were written gave a detailed overview of the cases that were being cared for by the staff working that shift. Midwives and doctors alike could easily see, at a glance, which patients were where, who was caring for them, and the details of their pregnancy and labour.

When Sylvia had started her Midwifery training, reading the board was like trying to read a foreign language. She would stop by the board on her way to start another shift and try to analyse the whole catalogue of abbreviations that were used by Midwives and obstetricians alone and chalked up on the board by each name. She frequently despaired of ever understanding it at all, but slowly, as her training progressed, she became familiar with all the abbreviated terminology.

For example, ARM written by a mother's name stood for artificial rupture of membranes. In other words, a woman who was to be induced into labour and as part of the proceedings would have the bag of waters that her baby was growing in ruptured or broken by using something called an amnihook, a long, thin plastic stick with a tiny hook on the end. This would be inserted into the cervix or neck of the womb and, locating with fingertips the membranes over baby's head, the Midwife would gently scratch with the hook until the thin membrane was broken, allowing the amniotic fluid in the sac surrounding baby to drain away.

This procedure was enough, often, to trigger the start of labour. Sometimes women were also given an intravenous infusion of a normal saline drip with the addition of a drug called Syntocinon. This would, over a period of hours, induce contractions and help to stimulate the mother into established labour.

Another abbreviation used was IUGR, which stood for intra uterine growth retardation. In this condition a baby did not grow at the normal expected rate inside the uterus during pregnancy. They were sometimes called 'small for dates' babies. A woman could reach full term, or forty weeks of pregnancy, and if baby was suffering from IUGR, only weigh three and a half pounds in severe cases. These babies needed very special monitoring during pregnancy and especially during labour as they often did not cope well with the stresses that labour imposed upon them.

It was the huge diversity of each mother's history, and the many different, unpredictable outcomes of the women's pregnancies and labours that so fascinated Sylvia. No two days on duty were ever alike. Some days she would go home on a complete 'high', having delivered two, or even three babies on one never-to-be-forgotten mammoth of a shift, where she ended up being three hours late coming off duty. Another day, having cared for a woman in labour whose baby had died during pregnancy, and another whose baby was to be adopted, she had cried bitterly in the changing-room as she donned her civvies to go home. There was much personal reflection on those days as she slowly adjusted to what it really meant to choose to practise Midwifery. She had read somewhere that Midwife stood for 'with woman', and she was truly beginning to understand the full meaning of the word.

Sylvia was working on the late shift, when she came on duty at eleven-thirty in the morning, the shift finishing at nine in the evening. There were lots of ladies who had been induced that morning, started off with their drips and an ARM up on one of the antenatal floors. A few hours later, as the drips and drugs worked their magic, women, who were by now in established labour, would be transferred downstairs to continue their labour on the labour ward suite.

Sylvia had been assigned to room one, which she knew housed a lady who spoke no English at all. She was from Pakistan, and this was her fourth baby. The report that the labour ward manager had given to the late shift staff coming on duty had outlined a number of problems associated with the lady's pregnancy and labour. She was only thirty-four weeks pregnant, a diabetic with a very large baby, who also indicated that her diabetic condition had not been very well-controlled during her pregnancy. She also had a very high blood pressure. To make matters worse, she had been in labour for eight hours and was not progressing. The last time the Midwife had examined her, her cervix had only dilated a centimetre or two, even with the help of a syntocinon drip.

The foetal monitor machine's print-out showed that the baby's heartbeat was very slow to recover after each contraction and the midwife in charge of the case had pointed this fact out to the senior

Registrar whom she had called in to give a medical assessment. Sylvia knew how high risk this case was for the mother and her baby. Even just one of her problems was enough to set huge alarm bells ringing. Diabetic patients could be very difficult to manage during pregnancy. Their diabetic status became very unstable, their insulin requirements fluctuated daily, and trying to maintain a normal blood sugar level was difficult to say the least. An uncontrolled high blood sugar level resulted in a large baby, so, as in this lady's case, there could be an infant who was premature but in severe uncontrolled diabetes weigh as much as nine or ten pounds. It was easy to think that, because of their size, these babies were fit and healthy, but the opposite was true. They needed very careful monitoring after birth as they suffered from all the problems of prematurity and a rapidly dropping blood sugar level as their placental source of high glucose was no longer available to them. The midwife in charge of the case was at her wits' end trying to get hold of an interpreter, but she was having very little luck. Sylvia could see how difficult it was for her, trying to explain to the lady's husband and her sister what was happening. To obtain informed consent on any needed decision, especially if an emergency arose and consent was needed immediately, was going to be well-nigh impossible.

The midwife in charge had called the senior Registrar in three times now. Baby was showing signs of foetal distress and the midwife knew that immediate delivery was needed. She had written in the notes, documenting her concerns and stating clearly that she had called for medical aid. The Registrar on duty was new to her but apparently a noted academic. He seemed reluctant to make a decision and instructed the Midwife to carry on monitoring. Sylvia busied herself wiping the labouring woman's brow with a cool, wet flannel, changing the absorbent paper sheets beneath her and taking regular pulse and blood pressure recordings as instructed, feeling very glad that she was not in charge of such a complicated case. The atmosphere in the room was draining emotionally, so different from the low-risk cases where, nine times out of ten a healthy baby was pushed into the welcoming arms of an excited and happy family and staff. Sylvia could see how very concerned the midwife in charge of the case was. Even her own very junior student status identified the many risk factors at play in the clinical history of the labouring mother in front of her and she wondered why she wasn't a candidate for theatre.

She was adjusting the pillows on the labour ward

bed and assisting its occupant into a more upright position when the door was pushed open and Sylvia's friend Rosie Smith pushed her head through the door.

"There's a vasa praevia in the bottom sluice if you can be spared to look at it," she said, directing her question to the midwife in charge, who nodded her consent as yet another dip on the foetal monitor pulled her over to scrutinise the print-out more carefully.

Sylvia joined her friend outside in the corridor.

"What's going on in there?" said Rosie and Sylvia gave her a running account of the problems and concerns as they made their way to the other side of the labour ward where awaiting their arrival in a plastic dish in the sink was a bit of a rarity. They both donned a pair of rubber gloves and carefully examined what was in front of them. What they were looking at was a placenta whose cord insertion was not central, as was the norm. It was located on the very edge of the placenta into very friable thin tissue. There was also one large blood vessel, seemingly detached from the rest that was embedded into the thin membrane surrounding the cord insertion. Sylvia gasped as she looked at it and understanding immediately the implications of the abnormalities in the afterbirth in front of her. If an ARM had been performed and the amnihook had pierced the blood vessel, catastrophic bleeding would have occurred, putting the mother and baby's life at risk. Attempting to deliver the placenta after delivery of the baby would also have created huge problems, as pulling on the cord to deliver it would have resulted in tearing of the cord attachment to the main body of the placenta, causing a torrential haemorrhage with the placenta still attached inside the mother's body. A maternal and foetal death could so easily have been the outcome for the mother whose afterbirth they were examining.

It was a miracle that the mother had wanted and requested a 'normal as possible' birth with no intervention during the third stage of delivery. She had wanted to 'do it all herself' and pushed her own afterbirth out, rather than the midwife pulling it out for her. That request had probably saved her and her baby's life.

Sylvia and Rosie leaned over the large white ceramic sink, the implications for what might have been sinking in. One of the advantages of working in such a large, busy unit was that they had a greater chance of seeing rarer or more unusual cases. Unbelievably, in the last year there had been three sets of triplets, an almost unheard-of statistic. A few months ago, Sylvia had been working on one of the postnatal floors when one of the triplet mothers was admitted after her Caesarean birth. The smallest baby weighed just over four-and-a-half pounds and the other two babies just less than five pounds and they were all in excellent health at birth. She watched as the door to the ward opened and three nursery nurses all pushing a cot each transferred the care of the babies to the postnatal ward staff. She still marvelled at how all of those babies had fitted inside that mother's body; one of the babies had been in a breech or bottom-down position inside the uterus, and she still lay in her cot with her legs extended and feet near to her neck as a consequence of her womb positioning. Over the next few days, the position of her lower limbs would right themselves.

Another experience that would stay with Sylvia for the rest of her life was seeing a set of Siamese twins who were joined from the chest down to the abdomen. Twins had been diagnosed quite early in pregnancy. Only after a delay in progress during labour had an emergency Caesarean section been performed, and staff and parents discovered the reason for the delay. It would have been impossible for the babies to be born vaginally, joined as they were. Neither of the babies survived the trauma of delivery, even though they were thirty-six weeks' gestation. They had only one heart between them, and nothing could be done to save them.

Having left the sluice and leaving the placenta in a plastic dish for other students to examine, Sylvia made her way back to room one only to be confronted with pandemonium. The labouring mum was crying out in discomfort and pain as staff were frantically transferring her onto a trolley. Her husband and sister stood to one side in the corner of the room, looking worried and directing a stream of questions to anyone who would listen but no one in the room understood them and the staff were so intent in manoeuvring as quickly as possible the trolley out of the room towards the theatre area that their pleas for information were lost in the flurry of activity. It was obvious that the progress of labour had taken a turn for the worse. Other staff were seen running towards the theatre doors, and an exodus of medical staff from the doctors' sitting-room at the same time, all heading in the same direction. An oxygen mask had been placed over the mother's mouth and she nearly fell off one side of the trolley, so uncontrolled had she become before Sid the porter managed to get the side bars up. He and another porter literally ran down the corridor to the theatre doors and disappeared inside. Sylvia was left standing in an empty room so she started to pack up the mother's belongings which she then took to the theatre doors, where Sid was pushing an empty trolley out of the doors.

"What's the news, Sid, is baby out yet?"

Sid's usual cheerful demeanour was missing. He ran a hand through his greying hair, shaking his head slowly.

"Doesn't look too good, Nurse Ayres. Looks bad and the midwives looked desperate."

Sylvia's heart sank. She knew that the theatre staff could from a standing start get a baby out of the uterus in seven minutes in an emergency, but it was always very touch and go. Some babies survived the seven minutes relatively unscathed due to the expertise of the theatre staff and, depending upon what degree of oxygen starvation that they were suffering from, others did not.

Sylvia went back to labour room one and began to strip the soiled linen off the bed, dumping it into a portable laundry bag that was on wheels. She pushed it into the sluice and then returned to the labour room and washed down with an antiseptic solution every available surface that was accessible. Even the legs and wheels on the bed and delivery trolleys were treated. She wiped and wiped, cleaning anything and everything with a vigour that was almost manic and knew that by doing so with such a frenzy was her way of not thinking about what was happening in theatre, it was a distraction to stop herself from thinking too deeply. She was on high alert for any sounds coming from the theatre area that would indicate that the emergency Caesarean Section was now over. All remained ominously quiet. After forty minutes, she could bear the suspense no longer. She went into the theatre changing-room and found the midwife in charge of the case sitting quietly, with tears on her face. She looked up as Sylvia entered. Their eyes met and she slowly shook her head. No words were exchanged. None were needed.

An hour later, Sylvia's support midwife, Sister Francis, talked through the case at length with her, outlining the problems and the decisions made during care. It was many months later when she overheard a conversation between two consultant obstetricians, one of whom had carried out the emergency Caesarean, that she understood more. She was sitting quietly in the sitting-room, alone, an unusual event. Next door in the doctors' sitting-room, the door was open so she could clearly hear the conversation that was occurring.

The case had resulted in an internal investigation

into the standard of care and decisions made. Both Midwife and Registrar had been reported to their respective governing bodies, the midwife to the Central Midwives' Board and the Registrar to the Royal College of Obstetrics and Gynaecology.

The midwife in charge of the case was severely reprimanded and struck off the register of practising midwives. Sylvia thought that this was particularly harsh. When she asked Mrs O'Neil about it, she explained that there was a protocol in place that dictated if the Midwife disagreed with a doctor's decision about care during labour, the midwife had a duty of care to overrule him if she felt that the decision made about care was the wrong one. She had the right to go over his head and discuss the case with a consultant, which she had failed to do, resulting in the death of a baby. Equally, the hospital management's procedures were scrutinised and changed because the Registrar on duty who had made decisions about the woman's care during labour had majored mainly in research, and was employed only as a locum to cover gaps when shifts were short. He was less experienced practically than his title suggested and should not have been working clinically on the labour ward.

Incidents like these really brought home to Sylvia

the responsibility that she, when qualified, would be accountable for when on duty. She was beginning to understand that she could not hand decisions over to someone else and exempt herself when she qualified. She looked down at her hands, the hands that were so instrumental in determining the decisions that she made, the hands that held the responsibility and outcome of life and death, and prayed that she never forgot what the whole essence of being a midwife was about: the safe delivery of a healthy mother and baby.

Chapter Fifteen

Charles Merton was struggling, a rarity for one of the most experienced consultants in the maternity hospital. He stood in the theatre changing-rooms, alone on a quiet Saturday night, also a rarity, which normally would be a blessed relief from the continual procession of planned obstetric cases and emergencies that poured through the doors of the theatre in a never-ending stream. Planning and carrying out seven or eight inductions a day plus attending to all the women who were admitted in spontaneous labour took its toll on all the staff and he was no exception. He was on the receiving end of all those cases that didn't go to plan and ended up with an abnormal delivery or complications. He'd been away on a five-day seminar at another hospital down south, much to his relief as his wife was becoming increasingly intolerant of his frequent absences. He was desperate for a break from her never-ending moaning about hardly ever seeing him. And she was right, they did hardly ever see other, they were like ships that passed in the night that never found tranquil waters to anchor in together.

Five days away, five days of peace, but five days of not being able to access the 'pick me up' that he was increasingly reliant upon to get him through the day. The small amounts of Pethidine that he on an ad hoc basis had been able to make use of for his own personal gratification were not enough to give him the calm, rosy outlook that guaranteed bonhomie for a good few hours. He was now unable to rely upon sloppy drug administration practices by Midwives who didn't look too closely at tallies in the Dangerous Drugs cupboard at the end of the day. Recently the Central Midwives' Board had, in line with national recommendations and the Hospital governing body, put in place new rules and guidelines about the administration and giving of Pethidine to labouring women. Two Midwives now had to check each ampule of Pethidine. The midwife giving the injection had to get another colleague to read the detail on the ampule and then count up how many ampules were left in the box in the cupboard. It was becoming impossible to get hold of the substance that initially he had complete control of, or so he thought, but which now had complete control over him. When the need hit him, which was becoming more and more often now, he began to experience physical symptoms that at first he thought were just small hypoglycaemic instances after working for eight hours with no break or food intake.

He noticed that he was sweating slightly and that his hands had a very slight tremor, and he started to sweat when it wasn't that warm. His reliance on Pethidine, an opiate and pain reliever, used almost continually throughout shifts by Midwives to relieve women's pain during labour, had insidiously crept up on him and now held him firmly in its grip. In its euphoric embrace, he had no doubts at all about his own ability to control his need and use, but like most addicts, his confidence and ability waned as the effects of the drug wore off, until he reached the point, as now, where he just had to feed his craving somehow.

He walked out of the theatre changing-room, and down the corridor towards the nurse station where a huge write-on screen on the wall by the desk showed the layout of the rooms on the labour ward. He scanned the information until he found what he was looking for. Women who spoke little English, who over four hours ago had had their first injection of Pethidine and could have a second dose administered by a Midwife if they needed it. He then had to find out which senior Midwife was the key holder for the drugs cupboard for that shift. They were responsible for checking with the requesting Midwife the number of phials of Pethidine left in the box before it was locked up again in the DDA cupboard. There was also a DDA cupboard in the anaesthetic room of the theatre where patients were first taken and anaesthetised before being transferred through an adjoining door into the theatre where the team of Obstetricians and Midwives were gowned up and ready to start their procedures. Pethidine and Morphine were also stored here and the key was usually pinned onto the inside pocket of the theatre Sister in charge that day.

When the gods smiled upon him, he would spy his chance when theatre was busy, go into the Midwives' changing-room and find the keys still pinned on the inside pocket, no longer needed as the anaesthetist would have prepared and drawn up all the drugs he would likely need before any commencement of surgery. It was an easy matter to take a full phial of Pethidine and write in the book and patients' notes that a patient had been given a dose of Pethidine. If he was lucky, he could manage to get a couple of phials over a week or two of busy shifts, one from each cupboard. He had spent some time copying a particular signature of a senior Midwife who used a bold, very joined-up script that was easy to replicate and he was becoming quite skilled at copying it. Shifts in the main were so frantically busy that as long as the tally between the DDA register and the number of phials in the box tallied, no one looked further. Different Midwives held the keys on different shifts, so there was no continuity of scrutiny. If one took the time to sit down quietly with the register and check off names and doses given against the number of patients going through the unit in twenty-four hours, discrepancies would be noted. Often, numbers tallied anyway as it looked from the notes that the woman had been given a dose of Pethidine which would account for how many were left.

He had no qualms about the cruelty of his actions as Midwives tried to calm and support women who were writhing in agony during the latter part of their labours with no pain relief coursing through their veins. As the victims he chose spoke little or no English, Midwives assumed that their patients were unlucky enough to have had a more painful labour than others or lower pain thresholds; it was just the way things were. Often they were viewed as women who were not well-suited to labouring or who were much more demanding than most women.

Rosie Smith was sitting in the Midwives' sitting-room on the labour ward enjoying what felt like the best cup of tea in the world. Her back ached, her feet ached, and she couldn't remember when she had last eaten anything. The seven planned inductions for the day, plus the usual admittances from home in spontaneous labour, had resulted in a nightmare of a shift. At one point, the labour ward had no beds vacant for about five hours and women were being delivered on the beds in the progress department just around the corner. Amazingly it was now quiet, a welcome lull before the labouring women of the Six Towns were admitted through the doors of the maternity unit. Rosie, Sylvia, and Penny had just four weeks to go before they took the final written examination in part two of their training. They would also have an interview with a senior obstetrician who would ask them questions about Midwifery and obstetric problems. She had, of course, no idea what she would be asked in either the written or oral part of her assessment and guesses of what might come up had been the talk of the coffee room for weeks now. Like a number of her colleagues, Rosie had adopted the 'drive and learn' method of revision. She had recorded on cassette tapes a huge variety of subjects, splitting them into antenatal, intrapartum, and postnatal segments. She then added five or six relevant facts that formed the basis for a fuller written answer, linked to a bewildering long list of clinical scenarios that she may be asked about. She played the cassettes as she was driving to and from the hospital, when off duty, and any other time she could manage.

Draining the last dregs of her tea, and wondering if she dared contemplate an almost unheard of luxurious second cup, she was abruptly brought back down to earth with the loud, insistent shrieking of an emergency buzzer that had been pressed somewhere on the labour ward. She stood up and quickly located the panel on the wall outside the door, which showed her which room had buzzed for help. Room six on the other side of the labour ward. She almost ran down the corridor and was relieved to see an experienced midwife beating her to the entrance of the room that was buzzing for help. She followed the midwife into the room and as she approached the patient and her husband, Rosie located the room's buzzer and turned off the ear-splitting cacophony.

Mrs Hussain and her husband had only recently arrived in England, and both spoke very little English. She had brought no case notes with her that gave any hint of any antenatal care she had received whilst living in India. It was her first child, and her labour was taking much longer than expected. The female family support that she craved so much was thousands of miles away and this cold new land, with its alien customs, did nothing to boost her confidence or senses of security. The pain of childbirth had come as a great shock to her tiny, childlike frame, and she felt certain she was going to die before this child made its entrance into the world. The injection she had been given hours ago had helped a bit, but she was desperate for some more. As the next contraction squeezed her abdomen to an unbearable peak of agony, she screamed out loud, the only way left to her of trying to ease the terror and pain that had reached unbearable heights. She writhed around the bed, scattering her covering sheet onto the floor, wailing out her fear and need for more pain relief in a great unintelligible stream of an Indian dialect not understood by any of the Midwives caring for her.

The midwife responsible for the case now had just come on duty, on a split shift, taking over from her colleague who had gone off duty for a few days. She opened the case notes and read to confirm what she already knew from the verbal report about her patient given to her recently by her colleague. Mrs Hussain had only recently been given a second dose of Pethidine and could not have any more for at least four hours, and only then if assessed and discussed with a doctor first.

Rosie helped her colleague to assist Mrs Hussain into a more central position on the bed. She plumped up her pillows, retrieved the fallen sheet and then under instruction from her supporting midwife tried to show Mrs Hussain how to cope with the pain of a never-ending stream of contractions by using well-tried breathing techniques. Rosie demonstrated them herself, taking great, slow deep breaths in, and exhaling in a longer controlled fashion, gesticulating to Mrs Hussain to do the same. Mr Hussain caught on quickly what Rosie was trying to do and copied Rosie's instructions as yet another contraction reached its crescendo. Mrs Hussain screamed out uncontrollably, her arms and legs thrashing violently as Rosie tried to stop her from falling off the bed.

"Try and get hold of an interpreter from the on-call list, will you?" This directed at Rosie by the midwife in charge, "Though I doubt you'll have any luck this late on a Saturday night."

Rosie disentangled herself with great difficulty from Mrs Hussain's frantic grip and went in search down the corridor for the information she required and a phone. Five minutes later she was back.

"Sorry Sister, there's only one interpreter on call and she's across at the accident unit dealing with a lady over there."

Mrs Hussain was still uncontrollably writhing on the bed, emitting a continuous high-pitched wail in her native language, which rose to a series of heartfelt sobs as yet another barrage of contractions assaulted her tiny frame. Rosie noticed, as did the Midwife with her, that Mrs Hussain was also making deep guttural sounds in her throat and bearing down, pushing vigorously.

"Open me up a vaginal examination pack, will you, Nurse, and let's see and hope she's fully dilated so we can get this baby delivered."

Rosie inwardly sighed with relief at the thought that delivery was hopefully not too far away. She was becoming distressed herself with Mrs Hussain's plight and the level of pain she was experiencing. She wanted it to be over as much as Mrs Hussain did and the sooner the better. She grabbed a sterile pack from one of the storage cubicles on the wall by the bed and pulled the stainless-steel examination trolley into position at the side of the bed, where she opened up the pack and dropped onto it a pair of sterile rubber gloves and some lubricating cream to aid the internal examination. Her supporting midwife scrubbed her hands, rapidly donned the gloves, and proceeded to examine her patient.

The look of dismay and concern on her colleague's face told Rosie that all was not well.

Mrs Hussain was definitely not ready to deliver her baby as her cervix or neck of the womb needed to be ten centimetres, or fully dilated, before her baby could be born. Rosie knew from experience with other cases that if a mother continually tried to push down on a cervix that was not fully dilated, it often resulted in the cervix itself becoming swollen and oedematous, which in turn affected its ability to dilate. Encouraging the mum to stop pushing before full dilatation was crucial in aiding the progress of labour. Clearing the used pack away, Rosie watched as the Midwife tried valiantly to dissuade Mrs Hussain from pushing, but to no avail. She became even more distressed, if that was possible, and such was the level of her distress, student and Midwife realised that medical intervention was becoming a necessity.

Rosie did her best to comfort Mrs Hussain, wiping her sweating brow with a damp cloth, turning her over onto her side and rubbing her lower back as Mrs

Hussain continued to bear down onto a cervix that was not going to release its cargo to the outside world. She could hear the midwife outside the door speaking on the telephone adjacent to their room, requesting immediate medical aid and the Consultant on call.

Five minutes later, as Rosie was helping Mrs Hussain to use Entonox, an analgesic gas piped in to each room and administered by a face mask, in an attempt to stop her continual pushing, the door was pushed open and the on-call Consultant strode into the room.

Charles Merton was feeling relaxed, alert, and in a good frame of mind. He didn't need to be given a detailed outline of the case he had been asked to assess, as less than an hour ago he had scrutinised Mrs Hussain's notes himself and then added a beautifully copied signature purporting to show the administration of an injection of Pethidine by a Midwife who was busy elsewhere. But of course he had to play the game. The Midwife in charge of Mrs Hussain's labour had entered the room behind him and gave him a detailed verbal report of her progress to date and the level of her maternal distress, which was completely swamping her labour progress. He agreed that delivery for maternal distress needed to be performed as soon as possible by performing a

Caesarean section and his senior Registrar would perform the necessary surgery. He murmured some soothing platitudes to Mrs Hussain and her husband as he leaned over her and, patting her hand, said,

"Let's get you delivered, won't be long now."

He left the hustle and bustle of the theatre and headed towards the lecture theatre where the flattering platitudes of a large group of junior medical students awaited him.

Rosie swiftly began to gather Mrs Hussain's belongings from her bedside locker into a plastic bag as the door swung open a few minutes later and two porters negotiated a trolley into the room. It was a tight squeeze, as whoever had designed the hospital had not given much thought to the need to transfer the patient from the bed to a trolley. Transfers were continuous to other areas of the hospital, almost hourly in this department, and the walls showed testimony to the bangs and knocks from the edges of trollies.

Sid had portered at the hospital since it had opened four years ago. Tall, with a thatch of salt-and-pepper hair and spritely in step, he was held in great affection by all the staff, and nothing was too much trouble for him. He was a mild-mannered, family man and loved his job. He manoeuvred the trolley with practised ease to the side of the bed, dropped the metal side of the trolley down with a clang and pushed it in close. Rosie helped him manoeuvre Mrs Hussain, with great difficulty, onto the trolley. She continued to cry out and thrash uncontrollably. Tears poured down her face as the pain as her labour became unbearable. Sid's colleague helped to manoeuvre the trolley out of the room as Rosie checked to make sure she had collected all of Mrs Hussain's belongings from the bedside locker.

Rosie turned and knocked Mrs Hussain's notes off the top of the locker with her elbow, scattering papers and blood test results onto the floor. The notes fell open onto the last sheet of written record keeping. She bent down to pick them up and placed them back onto the top of the locker, ready to push the blood test results into the flap at the front of the notes where they were normally stored. She scanned the notes briefly to make sure the records were up to date before taking them to join Mrs Hussain in theatre and noticed something odd. She peered more closely at the page. Rosie was a stickler for accurate record keeping. She had seen what happened to Midwives who had poor record-keeping skills and couldn't prove what care they had given - suspension from duty, investigation and disciplinary action.

The signature of the midwife who had given Mrs

Hussain her last injection of Pethidine was clearly written in red ink, dated, timed, and amount given. Nothing wrong there, all as it should be. Except for the timing. Rosie knew that the midwife in question couldn't have given the injection to Mrs Hussain at the time stated in the records. True, she had been caring for Mrs Hussain right up to the time before the injection was given. But then she had received a phone call that her mother was ill. She had gone off duty immediately, at least twenty minutes before the records stated she had given the injection. Rosie knew the exact time the midwife had left as she had hugged her as she left the labour ward, before going for a coffee break herself. She looked at the signature. She closed the bulky notes, tucked them under her arm, grabbed the bag of belongings, and hurried along the corridor to theatre where she knew the staff would be waiting for them, a worried frown on her usually cheerful face.

Chapter Sixteen

There was a loud scraping of chairs being pushed back as the room full of student Midwives stood up in deference to the arrival of Mrs O'Neil. She swept through the doors like the tour de force that she was and walked to the podium, a raised platform at the front of the classroom. Looking over the rim of her glasses at the large group in front of her, she ruminated on how far they had travelled both personally and professionally in the two years of their training. As well as getting to grips with the sheer volume of academic study and practical application, many had fought through personal trauma and tragedy during their two years with her. Marriage break ups were not uncommon as the maturation process of dealing so intimately with life and death on a daily basis changed naïve young women into strong, capable professionals who had very different outlooks on life at the end of their training. Friendships they had nurtured in their lives before midwifery sometimes withered and died as the students relied more and more on each other and not outsiders to bolster and support themselves and each other when times became tough. One student had been grief-stricken at the loss of her first child, aged just eighteen months with meningitis, and there were always students in every set she had taught who left because they found the long shifts and workload just too much to handle. Her eyes rested for a moment on the group of eight students sitting at the back of the classroom. They were the first set of direct-entry students where not one of them had left, the first group in her memory to have all stuck it out and stuck together.

She had called a number of groups together for a final briefing in the large classroom just a few days before they would be exposed to the trauma of their written and oral examinations and tensions were high. There had been the usual last-minute panic by students who had not yet completed their required forty deliveries; those who had not yet performed all their confidence cases and still others who had not completed all their required competencies. All fairly standard at this stage of the game.

Banging the blackboard eraser down hard onto the desk in front of her to gain their attention, the room fell silent. She motioned for them to sit.

"In a few days' time the pinnacle of all your hard work will be upon us. You have spent the last few months working through old examination papers to give you a flavour of the range of subjects you may be tested upon. I can't tell you what you will be asked, but often post-partum haemorrhage, hypertension during pregnancy, premature labour, and obstructive labour will, I am sure, be on that paper somewhere."

She paused for a moment as murmurs erupted and worried faces appeared from those students who now knew they had even more revision to complete over the next few days.

"You are all capable and competent students who have worked hard to get to where you are now, and I see no reason at all that would lead me to believe that any of you will fail. Remember, read the questions carefully at least twice, and remember to answer the question asked, not the question you think they asked!"

With a rare twinkle in her eye, she looked to the back of the room and said, "And who knows, Miss Jones, you may even get asked about the broad ligament!" at which the room erupted into laughter, easing the tension momentarily.

Two weeks later, in a very large regional teaching hospital complex forty miles away, eight young women sat with many others in a lecture theatre and turned over on the desk in front of them their final written examination paper. It would be followed by a face-to-face viva with a consultant obstetrician.

Sylvia looked at the questions, read them and then read them again. She thought about the last two years, the difficulties, the stress, the at times overwhelming emotions that threatened to engulf her. The journey she had embarked on had changed her profoundly. The strength and endurance of the women who had travelled through that journey with her would stay with her forever. She fully understood, finally, the definition of Midwife, 'with woman'. She took a deep breath in to steady her nerves and, with Mrs O'Neil's last words still reverberating in her ears, she put pen to paper and started a chain of events that would come to dominate the rest of her life.

Mrs Annie O'Neil, Senior Midwife Tutor

ABOUT THE AUTHOR

Sylvia Baddeley is a retired Midwife with forty-plus years of clinical practice. The death of her sister-in-law from a rare ruptured aortic aneurysm the day after her daughter was born was the catalyst that had driven her to enter the world of Midwifery.

Her career spans a journey that includes pioneering Aquanatal classes in the UK and lecturing locally, nationally and internationally at a number of Midwifery conferences as well as teaching exercise to music classes as part of her Midwife role. She acted as advisor to London Central YMCA's video on exercise during pregnancy and published a book called Health Related Fitness During Pregnancy. She was also Midwife advisor on Desmond Morris's video called Babywatching.

Throughout her career she published many articles on exercise during pregnancy in Midwifery journals. She qualified as an aromatherapist, body masseur and reflexologist as well as becoming a baby massage instructor and integrated all of these skills into her Midwifery practice. Her work in a local Sure Start programme offered opportunity for multi-agency working and the development of her role as a Bonding and Attachment Specialist Midwife for which she was invited, with others, to afternoon tea in the gardens of Number Ten, Downing Street, to celebrate achievements. Sylvia is also a familiar voice on local radio.

Printed in Great Britain
by Amazon

28090332R00129